STOP DYRETTE:
THE JOSEPHUS CONSPIRACY

DAVID GARRETT

dizzyemupublishing.com

DIZZY EMU PUBLISHING
1714 N McCadden Place, Hollywood, Los Angeles 90028
www.dizzyemupublishing.com

Stop Dyrette: The Josephus Conspiracy
David Garrett

First published in the United States
in 2021 by Dizzy Emu Publishing

dizzyemupublishing.com

STOP DYRETTE:
THE JOSEPHUS CONSPIRACY

DAVID GARRETT

FADE IN:

INT. MAG'S SECOND FLOOR WALK-UP - PRE-DAWN

Apartment fitted out with early 1970's era furniture,
appliances and decorations. Notably, its tech-free

MAG'S (22) is sleeping. An analog alarm clock rests on a side
table. Her eyes suddenly open. She wears an expensive but
worn out 1970's era designer T-shirt.

She sits up suddenly and surveys the room, then looks at the
analog watch on her arm. She turns off the alarm clock on the
side table.

Slipping out of bed, she pulls the bedroom curtain aside and
cautiously peeks out onto the street below. Nothing is
moving. Then, she heads for the kitchen.

INT. MAG'S SECOND FLOOR WALK-UP

Mag's hastens across the kitchen into the living room to her
apartment door that exits onto the stairwell. Many locks
secure the door. She checks them all to make sure they are
fastened.

Cat-like she moves to a living room window covered by a
curtain. Squatting down, she peeks out through the curtain
onto the street below. Nothing is moving.

Standing up she moves to the kitchen for breakfast. She gets
out her 1970's era bowl, spoon, and cereal box and
meticulously arranges them on the table.

She prepares to sit but then hesitates and disappears back
towards the bedroom. Moments later, from the bathroom, the
sink runs.

Mag's explodes from the bedroom dressed for the day in trendy
present day clothing. She carries her smartphone connected
through a cable to a small electronic box. She also carries
her tablet.

She arranges the electronics on the kitchen table and sits
down. She swaps out the smartphone for the tablet on the
cable. She pops a cartridge battery into the electronic box.

Then, she switches on the electronic box. It has a number of
controls and gauges which light up. It looks homemade but
expensive and well built.

She checks the gauges then props up the tablet in front of her to watch but doesn't turn it on.

Instead, she gets a 1970's era milk bottle from the refrigerator and sits down. She fills her bowl with cereal and pours the milk. She then grabs the cereal box and starts relishing the illustrations on the back.

Moments later she shifts her attention to the tablet. Turning it on, she finds an app labeled, "Dyrette Watch". She clicks it.

An app opens up. Mags scrolls through a menu of video clips. Finding one, she clicks.

ZOOM TO TABLET SCREEN

EXT. AFFLUENT EUROPEAN NEIGHBORHOOD - DAY

SUPERIMPOSE: MUNICH SUBURB

PEDESTRIANS gather around a fallen MIDDLE-AGED MAN (60s) on the sidewalk. He is clutching his chest, having a heart attack.

Sirens wail as an ambulance rushes up and stops at the curb. TWO PARAMEDICS jump out. One carries an ELECTRONIC WAND with an LED indicator and a medical bag. The other carries a kit which holds heart attack paddles.

They rush over and kneel by the fallen man. One paramedic raises the paddles. The other paramedic with the wand then passes it over the victim's heart. The wand's LED indicator flashes red.

With shock and disdain on their faces, the two paramedics pack up their equipment and leave.

Pedestrians stare down at the man gasping for air, then slowly drift off. An old lady, in her sixties, remains. The man looks up at her, eyes pleading for help. After a moment, she shakes her head, and then slowly walks off.

The dying man's face contorts in agony as his face turns blue.

ZOOM ENDS

INT. MAG'S SECOND FLOOR WALK-UP - KITCHEN

Distraught fingers quickly scroll through the menu of video clips a second time. Finding another one she clicks. She watches.

ZOOM TO TABLET

EXT. RIO DE JANEIRO - DAY

SUPERIMPOSE: RIO DE JANEIRO

Downtown coastal traffic during rush hour.

INT. RIO DE JANEIRO GROCERY STORE - DAY

A BRAZILIAN MOTHER (20) with TWO TODDLERS puts her last item, a bag of potatoes, into her shopping cart. She tentatively approaches the check-out kiosks. On her way, she passes through an overhead security "reader." An LED indicator on it flashes red.

A male STORE EMPLOYEE (40s) casually detains the mother. He gestures to the flashing red light.

She motions to her two toddlers who are sniffling. The Store Employee shakes his head, stubbornly refusing to let her purchase the groceries.

Other shoppers pass by looking at the woman with disdain as they make their purchases.

ZOOM ENDS

INT. MAG'S SECOND FLOOR WALK-UP - KITCHEN

Again, Mags hastily scrolls through the menu of video clips. Finding another one she fumbles momentarily and clicks. She rights the tablet and watches.

ZOOM TO TABLET

INT. HONG KONG HIGH RISE OFFICE BUILDING - DAY

An ELDERLY WELL-TO-DO COUPLE (70s), sit before a REAL ESTATE AGENT (50) at his desk. The downtown skyline is seen in the background through a large picture window.

The Real Estate Agent slides papers across the desk to the couple to sign. He then presses the intercom button on his desk phone.

                    REAL ESTATE AGENT
                 (in English, into
                  intercom)
          Kiki, please bring in the device.

He then turns to the couple and speaks to them in Chinese with English subtitles.

                    REAL ESTATE AGENT (CONT'D)
          A formality, you understand.

With a stone-cold face, KIKI (25) enters the room and waves a wand over the couple's chests. The wand's indicator flashes red.

The Real Estate Agent sees the flashing light and quickly gathers up the papers. The couple rises to leave as their faces turn red with embarrassment.

ZOOM ENDS

INT. MAG'S SECOND FLOOR WALK-UP - KITCHEN

Mags hesitates a moment absent mindedly twirling her cereal spoon. Then she again quickly scrolls through the menu of video clips. Finding another one an indecisive finger clicks it. She props the tablet up and watches.

ZOOM TO TABLET

EXT. RURAL VILLAGE - HORN OF AFRICA - DAY

SUPERIMPOSE: HORN OF AFRICA

A POOR MAN (40s) and his YOUNG SON (pre-teen) pull a tattered cart half full of vegetables to a local market. The market comes into view.

It's a filthy and rundown but busy market swarming with people. Loud, boisterous chattering is heard. Numerous carts and stands full of agricultural items are on display for sale by FARMERS AND MERCHANTS.

As the Poor Man and his Son get closer and see a spot they can move into, TWO SOLDIERS with machine guns detain them. Uncomfortable smiles cross their faces. The man shows his papers.

ONE SOLDER (24) inspects the paper and vegetables and then
nods to the SECOND SOLDER (19), who pulls out a wand and
passes it over the Poor Man's chest. The wand's LED indicator
flashes red.

                    POOR MAN
               (to soldiers)
          Please let my son and I pass!

                    ONE SOLDER
               (in African language,
                subtitled in English)
          No wafer, no selling for you.

ZOOM ENDS

INT. MAG'S SECOND FLOOR WALK-UP - KITCHEN

Slowly unplugging her electronic gadgets Mags returns them to
her room. She emerges momentarily tucking her smartphone into
a pocket. She crosses to her front door to exit into the
stairwell.

But before getting there she again squats down and peeks
through the living room window onto the street below. Nothing
is moving.

Standing she pulls on her hooded jacket. She moves to the
front door and begins to methodically unlock it but then
hears something.

                    MAGS
          Is that you MRS. BRADEY (63) ?   *

                    MRS. BRADEY (O.C.)   *
          Yes, dear.

INT./EXT. STAIRWELL - CONTINUOUS

Mags opens the door and is confronted with her landlady, Mrs.
Bradey who is wearing outlandish 1970's era clothing. She is
sweeping the stairs with an vintage broom. Mrs. Bradey
appraises Mags.

                    MRS.BRADLY
          That's cute, dear.

                    MAGS
          Not really. You're cute though.

Mags descends the steps. She arrives at the landing and
starts to set out then hesitates.

Pulling the hood on her jacket over her head, she quickly surveys the neighborhood. Nothing is moving. She sets out.

EXT. MAJOR CITY - GENTRIFYING NEIGHBORHOOD - DAWN

Mags hurries down a street lined with mixed residential and commercial properties. She continuously surveys her surroundings but sees nothing moving.

Dawn breaks. She sees the first rays of the sun rising over the buildings. She stops and lowers her hood. Her shoulders relax. She resumes her walk at a slower pace.

Moments later a car with tinted windows begins following Mags slowly at a distance. She senses it. Her shoulders tense. Her pace quickens.

Subtly looking over her shoulder, Mags confirms she is being followed. She raises her hood and quickly turns down an alley.

EXT. ALLEY - MORNING

Mags looks back. She sees the same car turning down the same alley. She breaks out into a run.

                    RADIO ANNOUNCER (V.O.)
          In other news, the saboteur of the
          artificial intelligence system
          known as Dyrette is still at large.
          An award of $2 million dollars has
          been offered by its developer,
          Hayward Enterprises...

The car speeds up. As Mags runs, she recalls a dinner date she had the night before...

INT. RESTAURANT - NIGHT - FLASHBACK

A waitress shows BRANDON (25) and Mags to their seats. Moments later, the two are seen smiling and chatting intently amidst the background noises and restaurant chatter.

END FLASHBACK

EXT. ALLEY - MORNING

The car tailing Mags stops in the alley. Two men, a silver-haired INSPECTOR ERAS (50) and tall, buff AGENT ARIEL (25), exit the vehicle and run after Mags.

Mags turns a corner into another alley.

EXT. SECOND ALLEY - MORNING

Mags hides behind a large dumpster, catching her breath. She
pulls out her cell phone and, in a whispered tone, says
something into it and throws the cell phone to the ground.
Mags smashes the cell phone with the heel of her foot.

The sound of running footsteps grow louder.

Mags grabs the now damaged cell phone and tosses it into the
overgrown grass alongside the alley.

Farther down the alley, the signage on a building reads:
"AQUAPONICS FARM."

EXT. SECOND ALLEY - MORNING

Inspector Eras and Agent Ariel turn into the second alley and
run after Mags. The same car trails them.

Mags grabs a trash can cover and hurls it at them, sending it
flying through the air. The two men bat it aside and continue
their chase.

Breathing heavily, Mags runs with all her might. She steals a
quick look over her shoulder. Just then, Mags trips over a
pothole and falls face-first to the ground.

Inspector Eras and Agent Ariel catch up with Mags. They grab
her by the arms and yank her to her feet.

                AGENT ARIEL
      There you are, Magusine. We've been
      looking for you.

She kicks and screams.

                MAGS
      I told you. I don't want to go with
      you!

Agent Ariel pulls out a syringe and injects Mags with a drug.
Her eyes roll back, and she falls limp. Inspector Eras
catches her in his arms.

The car with tinted windows pulls up. Agent Ariel opens the
back-passenger door, and Inspector Eras places her in the
back seat.

INT. CAR WITH TINTED WINDOWS - MORNING

Inspector Eras and Agent Ariel quickly climb in and sit on
either side of Mags.

Agent Ariel places a hood over Mags' head. Inspector Eras
leans forward to speak to the DRIVER (60) of the vehicle.

                    INSPECTOR ERAS
               (in a thick Israeli
                accent)
          Drive on.

The vehicle roars off.

Mag's head slumps back on the headrest. Blackness.

EXT. ISRAEL BEN GURION AIRPORT - NIGHT

A private jet lands. The signage reads: "BEN GURION AIRPORT."

Inspector Eras and Agent Ariel discreetly guide Mags out of
the jet and onto the runway. With the hood now off her head,
she looks groggy, walking unsteadily. As they drag Mags
towards the awaiting car, she attempts to stomp on the toes
of Inspector Eras but misses her step.

Agent Ariel stands guard, shielding Inspector Eras from view
as he slips the hood back over Mags' head. He then guides her
into the awaiting car.

INT. ISRAELI INTELLIGENCE HQ INTERROGATION ROOM - NIGHT

Mags is strapped in a chair with ankle and wrist restraints.
The room is sparsely furnished with a bank of high intensity
LED lights hanging over her head. Agent Ariel comes up to her
and lifts the hood off her head. She rouses. Inspector Eras
paces in front of her.

                    INSPECTOR ERAS
               (in a thick Israeli
                accent)
          Magusine Cohen.

                    MAGS
          Where am I?

Mags violently throws up on the floor.

                    INSPECTOR ERAS
          You are in Israel.

EXT. MAJOR CITY - DOWNTOWN STREET - DAY

It's downtown rush hour. There is a cacophony of street noise
at crowded intersections.

EXT. MAJOR CITY - URBAN OUTSKIRTS - DAY

Located in the depressed-looking outskirts of an urban area
is a large greenhouse. The signage on it reads: "AQUAPONICS
FARM."

Parking lot surrounds the greenhouse and connected farm
office. There's an alley in the rear. A truck parks.

INT. AQUAPONICS GREENHOUSE PRODUCTION SPACE - DAY

The lush green interior of an aquaponics farm. Quiet, serene.
WORKERS here and there check on the produce being grown.
Mechanical harvesters slowly move over rows of lettuce.

BEN (26) and EMILY (22) burst through the door of the
attached farm office into the production space.

                    EMILY
               (to Ben)
          Yes, I am concerned. Mags was
          supposed to be here hours ago.

INT. ISRAELI INTELLIGENCE HQ INTERROGATION ROOM - NIGHT

Mags is still strapped down in a chair. Inspector Eras paces
in front of her. He holds up a BIOMETRIC COMPUTER WAFER.

                    INSPECTOR ERAS
          You are the inventor, are you not?

                    MAGS
          What? No.

                    INSPECTOR ERAS
          Ariel, come in here.

After a moment, Agent Ariel enters with an electronic
hypodermic needle in hand. Mags wiggles hard against her
restraints. Agent Ariel calmly injects Mags in the back of
the neck.

                    INSPECTOR ERAS (CONT'D)
          You will feel better. Our
          intelligence observed you at the
          manufacturing location, I think.

Inspector Eras holds up surveillance photos.

                    MAGS
          My uncle's facility.

INT. AQUAPONICS GREENHOUSE - ATTACHED OFFICE - DAY

A desk with a large computer display on it. Nearby, an
elaborate computer server is on a rack with wires running to
a control panel and then out into the farm production area.
Through a window two flower pots are seen on a ledge.

                    EMILY
          Should we call her family? Her
          uncle maybe? It's not like Mags.

                    BEN
          Are you nuts? You want him to find
          us?

A warning alarm goes off. Emily looks through the glass
windows on the door to the production area.

                    EMILY
          It's down.

Ben looks at the server. It's flashing. Emily watches as Ben
placidly walks over and whacks the server on its side like
he's done it many times. The alarm stops. The flashing stops.

Emily looks again through the glass windows on the door to
the production area. The farm mechanics resume in the
production area.

                    EMILY (CONT'D)
          Back on.

EXT. MAJOR CITY - HAYWARD ENTERPRISES - DAY

An office building with tinted windows.

INT. HAYWARD ENTERPRISES - HAYWARD'S OFFICE - DAY

HAYWARD (55), stern-looking, works at his desk surrounded by
hi-tech conveniences. His henchman, LARRY (35) and GEOFFREY
(48) stand nearby.

A robot ambles over, holding a cup of coffee in its
mechanical claw. It attempts to hand Hayward the cup but ends
up spilling a little coffee on the desk.

Hayward violently pushes the robot over onto its back. Larry laughs. The robot exhales a sound of misery. Hayward shrugs, then signals to Geoffrey.

An ARTSY MARKETING EXECUTIVE steps forward and presses a button on a remote.

A video screen rises, and the promotional video plays.

ON VIDEO SCREEN

A male TV HOST (55), dressed as a lab tech, stands before a BOY (8) and GIRL (7) and the TV STUDIO AUDIENCE.

                         TV HOST
          This new state-of-the-art product
          is called "World Heartbeat." It's
          an implantable biometric wafer that
          communicates through "IoTs" to
          bring the convenience of the
          internet to its wearers.

PARENTS of the boy and girl stand by. The TV Host holds up a wafer in front of the children.

                         TV HOST (CONT'D)
          Looks almost like a piece of your
          mom's jewelry, don't you think?
          See?

                         GIRL
          Pretty!

                         TV HOST
          Your parents will be pleased to
          know only medical grade metals were
          used in its construction.

The parents smile.

                         TV HOST (CONT'D)
          No larger than a dime. Painlessly
          placed just below the skin near a
          person's heart. Like a shot at the
          doctors.

                         BOY
          I don't like shots.

A titter of laughter ripples through the audience.

                         TV HOST
          No one does. But we all need them
          to stay healthy, don't we?

The parents turn to each other and nod. So does the audience.

                    TV HOST (CONT'D)
          Right. And, it works in tandem with
          the Internet of Things.

The Girl stands on tip toe and whispers into the TV Host's
ear.

                    TV HOST (CONT'D)
               (repeating)
          What's the Internet of Things?
               (beat)
          Why, "Things" or gadgets all around
          us that speak to the internet for
          us!

An illustrative cartoon video on a screen behind them begins
to diagram how the wafer connects to the internet through, an
IoT.

The Boy waves to the TV Host and whispers in his ear.

                    TV HOST (CONT'D)
          Right. Clever boy. They are called
          IoTs, for short. Your wafer talks
          to these "things" letting them know
          you are there and giving them
          instructions on your behalf. IoTs
          then work with Dyrette on the
          internet to accomplish their tasks.

          YOUNG GIRL   YOUNG BOY
What's Dyrette?   What's Dyrette?

Audience members lean in eagerly to listen.

                    TV HOST
          Dyrette is the artificial
          intelligence or brains on the
          internet that helps us use it
          safely. How wonderful is that!

Cheers and clapping erupt in the audience.

                    TV HOST (CONT'D)
          Would you like to see some
          examples?

The Boy and Girl vigorously nod, causing their parents smile.

A video clip montage runs on the screen behind them,
illustrating the examples.

                    TV HOST (CONT'D)
          For example, it can open locked
          doors for people that have
          permission to enter.

The video clip shows GUESTS arriving.

                    TV HOST (CONT'D)
          And, keep bad people out.

The video clip shows TOUGH LOOKING MIGRANTS stopped at a
border crossing.

                    TV HOST (CONT'D)
          Your wafer working through an IoT
          can communicate important and
          complex medical information about
          you to your doctors when you get
          sick.

The next video clip shows a DOCTOR looking at a screen with a
medical history.

                    TV HOST (CONT'D)
          It can also help your parents find
          you if you get lost.

The Girl giggles. The Boy looks defiant.

                    TV HOST (CONT'D)
          And it can help our crops grow with
          just the right amount of water.

The video clip shows sensors pop up in a field of corn. And
LED on one turns green and the water sprinklers start.

                    TV HOST (CONT'D)
          Here's an example your parents
          might like.

The video clip shows mobile robots roam about mysteriously
bringing their host's GUESTS their drinks at a dinner party.

                    TV HOST (CONT'D)
          There are endless ways Dyrette and
          its wafers can help you.

INT. ISRAELI INTELLIGENCE HQ INTERROGATION ROOM - NIGHT

Mags is still tethered to her chair. Inspector Eras sits and
makes himself comfortable. An agent stands by observing.
Unhurried, Inspector Eras toys with a wafer.

                    INSPECTOR ERAS
          Why then, do you work for him?

Mags drops her head and declines to answer.

                    INSPECTOR ERAS (CONT'D)
          A simple question.

Mags groggily stares at Inspector Eras, who looks placid.

                    MAGS
          I quit. ...don't care about
          anything anymore.

Mags slumps over exhausted. Inspector Eras nods to Agent
Ariel who then removes the restraints from Mags. A FEMALE
AGENT enters. Agent Ariel and Female Agent assist Mags out of
the chair. She struggles to walk.

                    MAGS (CONT'D)
              (mumbles)
          ...don't care.

BEGIN FLASHBACK:

INT. MAJOR CITY - CATHOLIC CHURCH - DAY

Mags sits with Brandon. A PRIEST at the front of the church
ceremoniously offers the "host," in a wafer shape, high above
his head. Mags cringes.

The Priest then gestures with his hands, inviting the
congregation to participate in the Mass. Soon after, people
start lining up to receive the host.

Brandon rises to join the que.

                    BRANDON
          Are you coming?

Mags shakes her head.

                    MAGS
          You know I'm Jewish.
              (to herself)
          At least nominally.

As Brandon joins the que Mags stares at him, appearing in
deep thought...

INT. MAG'S CHILDHOOD HOME - SEDER DINNER - NIGHT

Mags sits with her BIOLOGICAL MOTHER and SIBLINGS having
Passover Seder. Their Seder is bland and routine, devoid of
meaning. Siblings disinterested and distracted. Part-way
through the meal, she gets up without explanation, shakes her
head in disillusionment, and leaves.

INT. MAJOR CITY - CATHOLIC CHURCH - DAY

Brandon returns to his seat beside Mags, having taken the
host. The CONGREGATION rises in unison. The priest blesses
them. They begin to exit.

EXT. MAJOR CITY - CATHOLIC CHURCH - DAY

Brandon and Mags exit the building. Off in the distance, Mags
spots a billboard sign advertising the benefits of the WORLD
HEARTBEAT, A BIOMETRIC COMPUTER WAFER.

Tears stream down Mags' face. Brandon comforts her.

Mags and Brandon watch families returning to their cars in
the church parking lot.

A YOUNG BOY (4) wanders around without his family, looking
lost and distressed. His dad pokes at his smartphone on the
"World Heartbeat" app and finds his son who is fitted with a
wafer behind a nearby vehicle, much to his relief.

Mags breaks down conflicted and upset.

END FLASHBACK.

INT. ISRAELI INTELLIGENCE HQ - GUEST ROOMS - NIGHT

Still looking groggy, Mags sits on a bed. The Female Agent
brings her a new set of clothes and toiletries, then points
to the bathroom in the corner.

INT. HAYWARD ENTERPRISES - HAYWARD'S OFFICE - DAY

The screen lowers. The Artsy Executive turn to Hayward and
Larry.

                    ARTSY EXECUTIVE
          Too cheesy?

                    HAYWARD
          Yes, but the public will love it.
          Idiots.

                    LARRY
          We'll show them why the American
          corporation is the envy of the
          world, right boss?!

Hayward groans.

INT. ISRAELI INTELLIGENCE HQ - INSPECTOR ERAS'S OFFICE - NEXT
DAY

Agent Ariel and Female Agent escort Mags into Inspector
Eras's comfortable office. She is rested, cleaned up, and
dressed in new clothes--but feisty.

Inspector Eras sits at a desk. He graciously beckons Mags to
sit. Inspector Eras stands, slowly paces near his desk, and
reads from a dossier.

                    INSPECTOR ERAS
          Dropped out of college. Appears you
          were failing.
               (beat)
          Started a coffee shop. It failed.

                    MAGS
          I closed it.

                    INSPECTOR ERAS
          Lived on the streets for a while.

Inspector Eras approaches Mags. He turns over one of Mags'
wrists to reveal illegal intravenous drug use.

                    INSPECTOR ERAS (CONT'D)
          Someone failed.

Inspector Eras sits down at his desk.

                    INSPECTOR ERAS (CONT'D)
          You are also a self-taught computer
          programmer; a coding prodigy, it
          seems.

Inspector Eras shows Mags a surveillance picture of herself
coding. He glances at the dossier again.

                    INSPECTOR ERAS (CONT'D)
          Sole apparent heir to your uncle's
          company, Hayward Enterprises.
          Interesting.

Inspector Eras holds up a wafer inquisitively again. Mags
stares at it in silence.

                    MAGS
          Are you after the reward? I'll pay
          you myself.

Inspector Eras shakes his head.

                    MAGS (CONT'D)
          Why did you bring me here?
               (shouting)
          Let me go.

                    INSPECTOR ERAS
          OK. As you wish. We will let you
          go.

Inspector Eras nods to Agent Ariel, who then restrains her.
The Female Agent throws a bag on Mags' head.

EXT. ISRAEL - DESERT - DAY

Scorching heat waves rise off the desert floor. Desolate. A
jeep carrying Agent Ariel, Female Agent, and Mags stops. The
Female Agent loosens the bag on Mags' head and pushes her out
of the jeep. She falls on the hard ground, moaning. Her hands
are still tied behind her.

Mags struggles to stand up. She shakes the bag off her head.
She sees the dust behind the jeep as it drives off at high
speed.

Mags looks around and sees barren stretches of desert. A
scorpion scurries by. She starts to walk one way then
hesitates and turns in another.

INT. AQUAPONICS GREENHOUSE - ATTACHED OFFICE - DAY

Emily walks up to Ben.

                    EMILY
          Then, where is she?

                    BEN
          Mags is a free spirit. She does
          what she wants.

                    EMILY
          I'm worried.

Emily rubs a cross on her necklace. She whispers a prayer.

EXT. ISRAEL - DESERT - NIGHT

Mags is collapsed on the desert floor, suffering from heat
exhaustion. Her lips are chapped from thirst. She sees blurry
headlights approaching in the distance and lifts her head.

Mags squints her eyes...

MAGS' HALLUCINATION

EXT. JUDAEAN DESERT - EVENING

A contingent of ROMAN SOLDERS is marching in formation across
a scorched desert. Sun is setting. Solders on the front row
carry fire torches to guide their way. Jerusalem off in the
distance.

SUPERIMPOSE: JUDEAN DESERT, 70 A.D.

                    NARRATOR (V.O.)
          The Romans began their conquest of
          the known world in 200 B.C. By the
          beginning of the first millennia
          they had reached Palestine.

EXT. STREETS OF JERUSALEM - NIGHT

SUPERIMPOSE: JERUSALEM

The Roman Solders continue their march through narrow
streets. Solders carelessly tip over vendor carts as they
march to stay in formation. INHABITANTS watch on stoically.

                    NARRATOR
          Like other nations before them
          Israel resisted the invaders from
          the Italian peninsula.

EXT. SECOND TEMPLE COMPLEX - NIGHT

SUPERIMPOSE: THE "SECOND TEMPLE"

Continuing in formation, the Roman Solders emerge from the
streets and reach the plaza surrounding the temple. The first
row holds fire torches ahead of them.

Boot footfalls stop uniformly. The Second Temple looms before them.

                    NARRATOR
          However, the Romans soon discovered
          the Jews were different.....

BACK TO SCENE

The jeep with Agent Ariel and Female Agent with its headlights on drives up. Mags shivers in the desert night.

Agent Ariel sits Mags up on the desert floor. Female Agent puts a bag on Mag's head and a blanket around her shoulders. Agent Ariel and Female Agent lift Mags up and throw her in the back of the jeep. They drive off.

INT. ISRAELI INTELLIGENCE HQ - INSPECTOR ERAS'S OFFICE -
NEXT MORNING

Agent Ariel and Female Agent escort Mags into Inspector Eras's office. She is cleaned up and dressed in new clothes, unrestrained.

Inspector Eras sits at a desk.

                    INSPECTOR ERAS
          Have a seat, Mags.

Mags plops down in a chair. Inspector Eras stands and slowly paces near his desk.

                    INSPECTOR ERAS (CONT'D)
          Shall we try this again? We are not
          so different you and I.

                    MAGS
          Do you have a name?

                    INSPECTOR ERAS
          Eras.

                    MAGS
          Eras, why I am I here?

Inspector Eras stands and paces uncomfortably. Agent Ariel encouragingly holds up a small cellophane wrapped box.

                    AGENT
          Shall I check?

Inspector Eras nods. Agent Ariel rips open the package. It contains a wafer detection wand.

Awkwardly, as though it's his first time, he waves the wand over Mag's heart. It flashes red. A corner turns up on Inspector Eras's mouth.

                    MAGS
               (sardonically)
          I despise the wafers.

Inspector Eras nods to Agent Ariel. Agent Ariel leaves, then returns with a leather dossier of over-sized papers. He hands it to Inspector Eras. Inspector Eras puts it on the desk. After a long pause,

                    INSPECTOR ERAS
          We need your help.

Inspector Eras puts on white gloves. He hands Mags a pair. Mags stands and slips them on. He reverently opens the dossier. It contains ancient documents on parchment.

Inspector Eras carefully begins to show Mags the pages, laying them out on the desk.

Inspector Eras points to the caption on the first ancient document. Mags picks it up carefully and looks.

                    MAGS
          The Diary of Josephus?

                    INSPECTOR ERAS
          You read Latin?

Mags shrugs. Inspector Eras hands her an English translation, several typed pages.

                    INSPECTOR ERAS (CONT'D)
          Here, in English. Newly discovered
          in Rome. Fascinating.

Mags returns to her seat and reads.

INT. ROME - COUNTRY ESTATE OF OLD JOSEPHUS - GARDEN ROOM - DAY

SUPERIMPOSE: ROME - COUNTRY ESTATE OF JOSEPHUS - 98 A.D.

A wealthy old man, OLD JOSEPHUS (60), in his sumptuous home is writing in his diary. A SERVANT brings him a cup of wine, then leaves.

                    OLD JOSEPHUS
          Many see me as a traitor to the
          Jewish people, my people, but that
          is not so. I was once a great
          general in the army of the
          Hebrews...

BEGIN FLASHBACK:

INT. NORTHERN ISRAEL - FORTIFIED CITY - DWELLING - NIGHT

SUPERIMPOSE: NORTHERN ISRAEL - 70 A.D.

A MOTHER (32) and DAUGHTER (11) prepare a package of food.
Kneeling before her eye level she says,

                    MOTHER
          Take this food to your father. He's
          working hard with OTHERS to fortify
          the city's walls against attack. We
          need to do everything we can to
          help him.

                    DAUGHTER
          Yes, mother.

She takes the package of food.

EXT. NORTHERN ISRAEL - FORTIFIED CITY - NIGHT

Behind the city walls, LOCAL PEOPLE are sharpening their
weapons, stacking bags of food, reinforcing stone walls, and
filling containers of water. They are preparing for an
attack.

With the package of food in hand, the Daughter hurries
through the city streets looking for her father.

Eventually, she finds her FATHER (33) and hands him the
package. He hugs her.

Nearby, a younger JOSEPHUS (30), in military uniform is
directing local people as they bravely reinforce their walled
city.

Josephus notices Father who is taking a short break with the
Daughter. He smiles.

Suddenly a flaming ballista ball hurdles over the city wall.
It crashes in to the father's chest. He collapses.

                    DAUGHTER
                  (screams)
            Father!

A LOOKOUT on the wall calls to Josephus.

                    LOOKOUT
            They are coming!

The ROMAN ARMY attacks the city. The Local People valiantly
fight back. Josephus leads them. His LIEUTENANT (30) assists
nearby.

After awhile, Josephus approaches the Lieutenant.

                    JOSEPHUS
            I need to move to the next city in
            their path. You take command. I
            hope to return with reinforcements.

The Lieutenant nods in agreement. Josephus steps behind a
barrier.

EXT. NORTHERN ISRAEL - FORTIFIED CITY - NIGHT - LATER

Josephus has disguised himself as a peasant.

Josephus's Lieutenant and a few LOCAL LEADERS watch as
Josephus slowly climbs through an escape door in the wall.

                    JOSEPHUS' LIEUTENANT
            Be safe, Josephus.

Just then, a MESSENGER hurries over and hands Josephus an
important note. He takes it and leaves.

Soon after, the Roman Army breaches the wall.

EXT. NORTHERN ISRAEL - DESERT OFF THE MAIN ROAD - NIGHT

Josephus walks in the desert off the main road, looking
discouraged. He glances down at the note in his hand. A town
appears in the distance. Morning breaks.

EXT. NORTHERN ISRAEL - CAPERNAUM - DAY

SUPERIMPOSE: CAPERNAUM

Josephus walks through Capernaum near the Sea of Galilee. He
finds a synagogue and enters.

INT. CAPERNAUM - SYNAGOGUE - DAY

Josephus observes ESSENE MONK ONE (50) and ESSENE MONK TWO
(50) inspecting an engraving on a stone in the wall in the
back of the synagogue. Josephus approaches them.

                    JOSEPHUS
          What does it say?

                    ESSENE MONK ONE
          It is a memorial of a visit to this
          synagogue by the Messiah several
          decades ago.

                    JOSEPHUS
               (sardonically)
          Country people.

                    ESSENE MONK ONE
               (with dignity)
          We have reason to believe
          otherwise.

Josephus examines them.

                    JOSEPHUS
          You are holy men.

                    ESSENE MONK TWO
          You look hungry. Will you take
          breakfast with us, brother?

Josephus nods. They depart together.

EXT. JERUSALEM - MILITARY FORTRESS ANTONIA - DAY

SUPERIMPOSE: JERUSALEM - ROMAN MILITARY FORTRESS ANTONIA

Soldiers are holding military exercises on the parade
grounds.

INT. MILITARY FORTRESS ANTONIA - MILITARY PLANNING ROOM - DAY

A map of Jerusalem sits atop a large table in a sumptuous
room.

VESPASIAN (65) strolls about with his son, TITUS (40). They
pause on a connected veranda overlooking the city. Vespasian
hands a scroll he is reading to a SERVANT, who then exits.

                    TITUS
Father, this means you may become
Emperor!

                  VESPASIAN
Perhaps. Rome. Full of lazy
bureaucrats, squabbling
politicians, and greedy wives.
    (beat)
These Jews, they also vex me,
Titus.

EXT. CAPERNAUM - ROAD TO THE SEA OF GALILEE - DAY

Josephus and the two Essene Monks walk down a road. The Sea
of Galilee comes into view off in the distance.

                  JOSEPHUS
The situation is grave. The Romans
will be here in a few days.

               ESSENE MONK ONE
Is there nothing more you can do?

EXT. WALLED CITIES OF NORTHERN ISRAEL - DAY

A MONTAGE of Josephus fortifying the walled cities in
Northern Israel.

               JOSEPHUS (V.O.)
My hope was to discourage them by
fortifying the towns in their path.
Now the Sanhedrin stops me.

EXT. CAPERNAUM - ROAD TO THE SEA OF GALILEE - DAY

Josephus holds up the note to show it to the two Essene
Monks.

                  JOSEPHUS
We could use your messiah now.

               ESSENE MONK TWO
Indeed.

               ESSENE MONK ONE
There is reason for hope.

               ESSENE MONK TWO
The scriptures reveal a messiah
will visit us twice.

END FLASHBACK.

INT. HAYWARD ENTERPRISES - HALLWAY - DAY

Hayward and his two henchman, Larry and Geoffrey, walk
rapidly down a hall. Hayward is frowning.

                    HAYWARD
          Any luck yet?

Larry and Geoffrey shake their heads "no."

                    HAYWARD (CONT'D)
          She must have found a way to hide
          from us. Developed new cloaking
          code on a server somewhere perhaps.

Larry and Geoffrey nod in agreement.

                    HAYWARD (CONT'D)
          If you idiots can't find Mags at
          least find me that server!

INT. AQUAPONICS GREENHOUSE PRODUCTION SPACE - DAY

Ben and Emily enter their aquaponics farm. The farm is in
disarray, burglarized. Irrigation tables are overturned.
They walk through the destruction, making way to the
connected office.

INT. AQUAPONICS GREENHOUSE OFFICE - DAY

Papers are everywhere. Ben checks the money drawer. He holds
up a fistful of dollars, bewildered.

Emily then points in shock at the spot where Mags' server
used to be positioned. Unconnected wires litter the floor.
Two flower pots can be seen through a window on a ledge.

                    BEN
          How did they find us?

                    EMILY
          I might have called her mother.

Ben groans. They hear a noise.

                    BEN
          I'm gonna take a look out back.

Ben passes through a door in the greenhouse office and steps out into an alley with overgrown grass.

EXT. ALLEY BEHIND GREENHOUSE OFFICE - DAY

Ben sees a cat knocking one of the flower pots as it jumps off the window ledge. The cat walks in the overgrown grass. He looks curiously at the ledge and at the pots. Then, Ben looks down and spots something.

EXT. SEA OF GALILEE - RESTAURANT - 70 A.D.

SUPERIMPOSE: SEA OF GALILEE - 70 A.D.

Humble seaside restaurant. Josephus and the two Essene Monks sit on rough benches with a table. The FISHERMEN done for the morning sit nearby. The RESTAURANT KEEPER brings a tray of fish and bread to Josephus and the monks. They eat.

                    ESSENE MONK TWO
          Permit us to tell you our story.

                    ESSENE MONK ONE
          As youths.

FLASHBACK:

INT. CLIFFS BY THE DEAD SEA - ESSENE MEETING CHAMBER - DAY

SUPERIMPOSE: THE DEAD SEA - 45 A.D.

Younger ESSENE MONK ONE (25) and Younger ESSENE MONK TWO (25) stand before the CHIEF MONK and TWO OTHER MONK LEADERS in the company of the ESSENE COMMUNITY.

                    ESSENE MONK ONE
               We have heard reports from people
               all over Israel who believe a
               person they have encountered is the
               true messiah.

                    ESSENE MONK TWO
               We compared these reports to the
               holy scriptures we were copying.

                    ESSENE MONK ONE
               And we think there is reason for
               hope.

Chief Monk shakes his head disapprovingly.

                    CHIEF MONK
          And what do we say to such as
          these, brothers?

                    TWO OTHER MONK LEADERS
               (in unison)
          Sacrilege!

                    ESSENE COMMUNITY
               (in unison)
          Banish them!

EXT. CLIFFS BY THE DEAD SEA - ESSENE PURIFICATION GROUNDS -
DAY

The two Essene Monks slowly walk through the grounds with
their packed bags. No one speaks to them.

                    ESSENE MONK TWO (V.O.)
          That day we arrived at the
          community "Mikva" to be cleansed
          one last time from our sins. But we
          were prevented by the brothers
          waiting in line.

THOSE BROTHERS IN LINE block the two Essene Monks, denying
them access.

                    ESSENE MONK ONE
               (to Monk Two)
          No need now, brother.

EXT. SEA OF GALILEE - RESTAURANT - 70 A.D.

Josephus stops eating his breakfast and looks up at the two
Essene Monks.

                    JOSEPHUS
          Why this reason for hope? How do
          you know it's true? All I have seen
          is an engraving on the stone you
          showed me, and an old one at that.

                    ESSENE MONK ONE
          Not outside living memory, however.
          Wouldn't you agree?

                    JOSEPHUS
          Perhaps. The carving itself attests
          its own date nearly 30 years after
          Herod's census; only a generation
          ago.

                    ESSENE MONK TWO
          A point well taken by you,
          nevertheless. It's true that the
          man we believe was the Messiah
          departed from us more than three
          decades ago.

                    ESSENE MONK ONE
          In rebuttal, however, note well
          that we began our investigation
          into the truth of the matter some
          25 years ago, when memories still
          lingered in our witnesses' minds.

                    ESSENE MONK TWO
          We have been making inquiries ever
          since that time; lo, these many
          years.

                    ESSENE MONK ONE
          First, we travelled to Jerusalem
          and Bethlehem.

                    ESSENE MONK TWO
          Then, to Nazareth.

                    ESSENE MONK ONE
          And now we are here in the Galilee.

                    ESSENE MONK TWO
          The testimonials about this
          remarkable individual are
          disquietingly consistent.

                    ESSENE MONK ONE
          Testimonials from those who knew
          the man personally and witnessed
          the signs and wonders he performed.

                    JOSEPHUS
          Why would signs and wonders attest
          to the matter? Conjurers are
          commonplace.

                    ESSENE MONK TWO
          We agree. But always for profit.
          The witnesses we questioned
          uniformly stated the signs and
          wonders he performed served no such
          purpose. Now we believe he did them
          simply so they would be seen and
          heard and thereafter be ascribed to
          him.

                    JOSEPHUS
          As a marker or signpost to be
          discovered by truth seekers such as
          yourselves, you argue?

                    ESSENE MONK ONE
          Verily. Here in this town we have
          spoken to several who attended the
          feeding of the 5000, as it is
          remembered, a miracle using only
          five loaves and two fishes to
          nourish a hungry crowd of
          thousands.

                    ESSENE MONK TWO
          And, the wine-making miracle at a
          wedding in Canaan. Still remembered
          with wonder by many of the bride
          and groom's then young guests.

                    JOSEPHUS
          Memories can be fallible, can they
          not? Witnesses can be bought; have
          bias.

                    ESSENE MONK ONE
          We agree. But not only witnesses
          attest to the messiah. There are
          other sources which establish the
          truth of this matter.

                    JOSEPHUS
          You are but misguided zealots.

The two Essene Monks match his gaze. Josephus gets up and
paces.

                    JOSEPHUS (CONT'D)
          My faith is more contemporary,
          pragmatic, at one with rationality
          of the Greeks.

                    ESSENE MONK ONE
          And yet, Socrates himself would
          agree with our method, what say
          you?

                    JOSEPHUS
          Socrates notwithstanding, I do not
          buy into signs and wonders as proof
          of the matter even if they are
          attested to by many.

Josephus sits again. A STOOPED-OVER MAN ambles by their
breakfast table.

                    ESSENE MONK TWO
          Brother, are you familiar with the
          stone engraving at the back of the
          temple?

                    STOOPED-OVER MAN
          Indeed, I am. I was an apprentice
          to the mason who carved it.

                    JOSEPHUS
               (demanding)
          Towards what end, the engraving.

                    STOOPED-OVER MAN
          A memorial of his visit.

                    JOSEPHUS
          Whose visit? Speak up.

                    STOOPED-OVER MAN
          The man who healed my father, then
          a leper. I was but a boy.

                    JOSEPHUS
               (to the Essene Monks,
                cynically)
          A healer? That is all?

The Stooped-Over Man looks at him curiously and then ambles
away.

                    JOSEPHUS (CONT'D)
          Truth of the matter? I think not.

                    ESSENE MONK TWO
          Truth as far as it goes. This old
          man adds his testimony to the many
          others who paid for the stone to be
          engraved. People who believed this
          man to be the messiah.

                    ESSENE MONK ONE
          And there is more to be considered,
          as we said.

                    ESSENE MONK TWO
          Namely, the comparison of
          testimonials such as this old man's
          with the holy scrolls concerning a
          messiah; our passion as young
          Essene monks.

                    JOSEPHUS
          Make your case.

                    ESSENE MONK ONE
          Please consider these correlations.

They pull out their scrolls.

MONTAGE: The two Essene Monks appear to be citing various
scriptural passages, gesturing with their hands as Josephus
listens to them attentively. Then, a specific reference.

                    ESSENE MONK ONE (CONT'D)
          The Old Testament talks about the
          messiah being pierced and raised up
          to suffer before the people.

                    JOSEPHUS
          Hearing that passage in Isaiah
          makes me recall the many painful
          crucifixions I have witnessed.

The two Essene Monks nod.

                    JOSEPHUS (CONT'D)
          Odd, sounds like you are describing
          a sacrificial lamb not a conqueror.

                    ESSENE MONK TWO
          Indeed, we are. But a conqueror
          nonetheless.

                    ESSENE MONK ONE
          The implications are confounding.

                    ESSENE MONK TWO
          Particularly concerning temple
          sacrifice.

                    ESSENE MONK ONE
          And, about the future.

                    JOSEPHUS
               (distracted)
          I must go to Jerusalem.

INT. AQUAPONICS GREENHOUSE OFFICE - DAY

Ben re-enters from the alley through the door in the
greenhouse office. He holds up a damaged cell phone. Emily
grabs it.

                    EMILY
          Hey! That's Mags's phone. The touch
          screen is cracked but let's see if
          it still works.

She attempts to unlock it fumble-fingered with excitement.
The second time she is successful.

                    BEN
          How do you know her pin?

Emily points to the server.

                    EMILY
          She told me. Mags set the phone up
          to run through the... well, what
          used to be over there on the rack.
          Remember?

Ben holds out his hand for the cell phone.

                    BEN
          I'm the tech guy.

Emily winces and gives the cell phone to him. He fiddles with
it.

                    BEN (CONT'D)
          Well, no internet coverage.

Emily points again sarcastically at the missing server. Ben
continues to tap on the cell phone. All of a sudden Mags'
voice is heard.

                    MAGS (O.C.)
               (recorded, out of breath)
          These guys from Tel Aviv asked
          me... I said 'no.' Now they're
          chasing me.

INT. HAYWARD ENTERPRISES - CONTROL ROOM - DAY

Hayward and his two henchman, Larry and Geoffrey, stand in a
control room with a map of the world projected on a glass
panel in front of them.

                    HAYWARD
          And the server?

Larry shrugs. Hayward scowls and turns his attention to the
map. He presses a button on a control panel. The map shows
all countries are shaded green except Switzerland, England,
and Israel which are shaded red.

                    HAYWARD (CONT'D)
          Stragglers who refuse our
          protection.

Hayward stares at the map then approaches it and slowly
traces his finger around Switzerland.

                    HAYWARD (CONT'D)
          Dyrette seems to be malfunctioning
          here, don't you think?

He nods to a naïve but eager-to-please TECHNICIAN (22).

                    HAYWARD (CONT'D)
               (in leetspeak, hacker
               language)
          Time for sploitzen!

                    TECHNICIAN
               (in leetspeak, hacker
               language)
          Roxsorz, sir!

The Technician codes. Switzerland flashes a warning signal on
the projection.

INT./EXT. GENEVA, SWITZERLAND - DAY

SUPERIMPOSE: GENEVA

MONTAGE: Clips which show the dystopian effects of unfettered
hacking. Traffic on the streets begins to snarl, cell phones
stop working, office computers go black, etc. A watch factory
grinds to a halt. A chocolate making factory malfunctions,
spilling chocolate.

INT. HAYWARD ENTERPRISES - CONTROL ROOM - DAY

A SECRETARY comes in.

                    SECRETARY
          Our sales manager in Switzerland is
          on the line.

Hayward picks up a phone. Switzerland is still flashing on
the projection. He listens nodding.

INT. AQUAPONICS GREENHOUSE OFFICE - DAY

                    EMILY
          She's sounds terrified!

Ben starts grabbing valuables and cash from the drawer.

                    BEN
          We can't stay here. He knows where
          to find us!

Emily ponders. She plays with the cross on her necklace.

                    EMILY
          We're going to Tel Aviv.

INT. INTELLIGENCE HQ - HALLWAY - NIGHT

Mags and Inspector Eras are walking together.

                    MAGS
          So why is this story about Josephus
          so important for Israel now?

                    INSPECTOR ERAS
          Some of us still believe a twice
          appearing Messiah is coming; even
          after 2000 years.

                    MAGS
          Seriously. How so?

                    INSPECTOR ERAS
          Our own investigation into the
          matter. We've taken a look at the
          evidence ourselves and studied the
          scriptures. We just don't know when
          the messiah will come.

                    MAGS
          Pretty important parameter.

                    INSPECTOR ERAS
          No date is given; perhaps on
          purpose. However, the scriptures do
          describe, however cryptically,
          several highly characteristic world
          conditions that will exist just
          before the messiah arrives. We see
          those conditions shaping up now.
          Dyrette and the wafers are part of
          that. We are convinced.

                    MAGS
          Is that why you kidnapped me?

                    INSPECTOR ERAS
          We knew you were involved with the
          Dyrette project but we weren't sure
          to what extent. We also knew that
          you had something to do with the
          wafers.

                    MAGS
          I see.

                    INSPECTOR ERAS
          Most importantly, we learned that
          you were estranged from your uncle;
          a textbook Intelligence Agency
          opportunity.

They walk on in companionable silence for a few moments.

                    MAGS
          My uncle thought I was naïve at
          first. His employees thought I was
          a spoiled brat. His two henchman
          treated me like a child.
               (beat)
          When I first raised concerns about
          the wafers, everyone thought I was
          just mad because I didn't get the
          credit I deserved for taking the
          lead coding Dyrette.
               (beat)
          Wanna know what really motivated me
          to sabotage Dyrette?

                    INSPECTOR ERAS
          You saw what was coming with the
          wafers?

                    MAGS
          Yes, but that was only the
          beginning of my concern. There are
          many ways my uncle could pervert
          the use of the Dyrette protocol.

After a few moments, Inspector Eras reaches out and softly
touches Mag's arm.

                    INSPECTOR ERAS
          Mags, will you help us to develop
          our own protocol so Israel can
          refuse to cooperate with your
          uncle?

Mags ponders.

INT. GENEVA, SWITZERLAND - AIRPORT - DAY

With their backpacks strapped on, Ben and Emily run down a hallway to their gate.

A SIGN READS: "WELCOME TO SWITZERLAND."

                    BEN
          They're canceling everything!

                    EMILY
          We have to make this connection!

They arrive at their gate.

A SIGN READS: "FLIGHT CANCELED."

Emily starts to cry. Ben comforts her. Emily bows her head in a quick prayer.

INT. HAYWARD ENTERPRISES - CONTROL ROOM - DAY

Hayward is holding a phone. He then signals a technician. The technician codes. Hayward, Larry, and Geoffrey watch the map. Switzerland flashes white and then turns green.

INT./EXT. GENEVA, SWITZERLAND - NIGHT

MONTAGE: Traffic eases. Order is restored to the watch factory. Ben and Emily get on the plane at the airport. Emily strokes the cross on her necklace.

EXT. TEL AVIV ISRAELI - AIRPORT TAXI PICKUP - NIGHT

Ben and Emily exit the airport arrivals area.

A SIGN READS: "BEN GURION AIRPORT."

Ben hails a taxi. They get in. It drives off.

INT. TEL AVIV ISRAELI - AIRPORT - TAXI - NIGHT

Ben and Emily sit in the back seat of the taxi.

                    TAXI DRIVER
          Welcome to Tel Aviv.

The taxi cab comes to an intersection. The Taxi Driver turns left. Emily looks at her cell phone.

                    EMILY
          Hey, my GPS says turn right. Go
          that way.

                    TAXI DRIVER
          You are looking for Magusine Cohen,
          are you not?

                    BEN
          What?

                    TAXI DRIVER
          I can take you to her.

INT. HAYWARD ENTERPRISES - CODING ROOM - DAY

The Technician is reading something closely on his screen. He
looks up at Hayward.

                    HAYWARD
          What?

                    TECHNICIAN
          That woman who called your sister
          yesterday to tell us about your
          missing niece... Her phone just
          popped up in Israel.

INT. AQUAPONICS GREENHOUSE - DAY

Brandon enters. The farm is in disarray. The lights are out.
He notices the broken windows. The place appears abandoned.
Water dribbles out of a tipped over aquaponics bed.

Brandon looks around and twitches his nose.

                    BRANDON
          Smells like rotting fish.

He picks his way through the debris.

                    BRANDON (CONT'D)
          Anybody here? Mags? Ben? Emily?

A feral cat screeches. He moves to the greenhouse office.

INT. AQUAPONICS GREENHOUSE OFFICE - DAY

Brandon enters. Sees more vandalism. He notices Mags' server
is missing. The cat runs by him and leaps out a window.

                    BRANDON
          Mags?

Brandon begins opening drawers and cabinets, looking for
clues. He finds a metal box and puts it on top of the desk.

Opening it, he finds a wafer in a "shielded" container, a
detection wand, and Mags' employee pass. He gazes at the
items. He then switches on the wand.

The wand signals red despite the presence of the wafer. He
opens the shielded container and removes the wafer. The wand
indicator immediately turns green.

Curious, he replaces the wafer in the container. The wand
indicator again turns red. He repeats the process.

Brandon inspects Mags' employee pass. Pondering, he puts the
wand, pass, and wafer container back in the metal box. He
turns to exit. He takes the box.

INT. ISRAELI INTELLIGENCE HQ - CONFERENCE ROOM - NIGHT

Ben, Emily and Mags are sitting at a conference table with
Inspector Eras, who has a notepad out in front of him.

                    MAGS
          ...they were using destructive
          'wiper' attacks, spear phishing,
          password spraying, and credential
          stuffing. They succeeded in taking
          control of entire networks that
          way.

                    INSPECTOR ERAS
          We experienced the hacking here as
          well.

                    BEN
               (interrupts)
          We got hit by ransomware.

                    MAGS
          Their automated farming system was
          totally dependent on the internet.

                    EMILY
          So we contacted Mags.

                    BEN
          We all went to high school
          together.

                    EMILY
          No, we didn't. You were 4 years
          ahead of us.

                    MAGS
          I brought my computer server to
          their farm and coded a simple
          artificial intelligence on it to
          protect them.

                    BEN
          Which would later become the coding
          base for Dyrette!

                    EMILY
          Excuse us a minute.

Ben and Emily get up and go into an adjacent hallway.

INT. ISRAELI INTELLIGENCE HQ - ADJACENT HALLWAY - NIGHT

Ben gets in Emily's face.

                    BEN
          What the heck is wrong with you?
          Who cares if I am four years older
          than you two?

                    EMILY
          I don't trust him.

                    BEN
          He's our host!

                    EMILY
          Why are you telling him about the
          code base?

                    BEN
          He's protecting us from Hayward!

                    EMILY
          He's a spy!

They return to the Conference Room.

INT. ISRAELI INTELLIGENCE HQ - CONFERENCE ROOM - NIGHT

Ben and Emily resume their seats at the conference table with
Mags and Inspector Eras.

                    MAGS
We set my server up between their
computer and the control panel
which handled the farm mechanics.

                    BEN
And it worked! Our own hacker-free
internet oasis.

                    INSPECTOR ERAS
How did your uncle get his hands on
your coding?

                    MAGS
He persuaded me to join the family
business which I agreed to do.

                    EMILY
Her parents were on her back about
it. She had to.

                    MAGS
I felt like I had found my people.
He had assembled this great coding
team.

                    INSPECTOR ERAS
A rare thing.

                    MAGS
The only other person I knew who
could really code was my friend,
Brandon.

                    EMILY
          (to Inspector Eras)
Her boyfriend, she thinks.

EXT. HOME OF MAGS'S PARENTS - DAY

A wealthy suburb outside of a MAJOR CITY. Brandon drives up a
long driveway on his motorcycle. He "revs" it loudly a couple
of times before parking. He removes his helmet and props the
motorcycle up on a kickstand.

The STEPMOTHER (50) of Mags opens the front door as he
prepares to walk up the elaborate steps. She holds a glass of
bourbon.

                    STEPMOTHER
I heard you. What do you want?

                    BRANDON
          I am a friend of your daughter
          Mags.

                    STEPMOTHER
          I suppose she is. I'm her
          stepmother, they say.

She takes a sip.

                    BRANDON
          ...trying to find her.

                    STEP-MOTHER
          She isn't here.

                    BRANDON
          You aren't worried?

                    STEP-MOTHER
          Traitor to the family as far as I'm
          concerned.

INT. ISRAELI INTELLIGENCE HQ - CONFERENCE ROOM - NIGHT

Mags, Ben, and Emily watch quietly as Inspector Eras jots
down some notes.

                    INSPECTOR ERAS
          What happened next?

                    MAGS
          Dyrette rolled out regionally in
          the Midwest, then nationally, and
          finally went international.

                    BEN
          A politician at the United Nations
          was helping her uncle cut through
          the red tape.

                    INSPECTOR ERAS
               (to himself)
          A false prophet?

                    MAGS
          When Dyrette became this big
          success, my uncle decided to take
          it one step further.

                    INSPECTOR ERAS
          The wafers?

                    MAGS
          Yes. He and I disagreed about the
          wafers so I left the company.

                    INSPECTOR ERAS
          But you suspected he'd keep
          pursuing it.

                    MAGS
          Right. We had to stop him. Even if
          that meant shutting down Dyrette
          altogether.

                    BEN
               (boasting)
          Which we did.

Emily groans.

                    INSPECTOR ERAS
          You shut down Dyrette?

Mags nods.

                    INSPECTOR ERAS (CONT'D)
               (to Mags)
          Why are you hiding from him now?

Mags nods, then glances at Ben.

                    BEN
               (interjects)
          Then the hackers went crazy again.
          No Dyrette. No protection.

                    MAGS
          Then, of course, he found a way to
          resurrect Dyrette.

Inspector Eras stands and paces the room.

                    INSPECTOR ERAS
          So now he is gaining control of the
          world--nation by nation.

                    BEN
          It gets worse.

                    MAGS
          He wants to implement this scoring
          system using the wafers where the
          quality of life you are allowed is
          based on your "conduct."

                    INSPECTOR ERAS
          If you do what they want, you get
          food and shelter, for example?

                    MAGS
          Right.

Inspector Eras ponders.

                    INSPECTOR ERAS
          And if we give in to your uncle, we
          risk our "faith freedom" among
          other things.

                    MAGS
          Faith freedom?

Alarms go off. Panels come up on the walls of the conference
room.

INT. HAYWARD ENTERPRISES - CODING ROOM - DAY

DR. FRANK PAULSEN (65), a U.N. Statesman, enters. Hayward
extends a warm greeting. Larry, Geoffrey, and the Technician
watch on in awe. A screen shows an aerial of London. They
watch.

INT. ISRAELI INTELLIGENCE HQ - CONFERENCE ROOM - NIGHT

BANK OF VIDEO SCREENS

News channels on. There's a video coverage of a dystopian
England. Chaos on the screens. Report after report. After a
while, the dystopia stops; suddenly, like a switch was
thrown.

BACK TO SCENE

Mags, Ben, Emily, AGENT ARIEL and Inspector Eras watch the
video screens in disbelief.

                    AGENT ARIEL
          Looks like England has capitulated.

                    INSPECTOR ERAS
          We're next unless we find a way to
          stop him.

                    BEN
          Can we try doing what we did at the
          farm?

                    MAGS
          We could scale it.

Inspector Eras nods. Mags rises and paces as she thinks.

                    MAGS (CONT'D)
          And then maybe take it one step
          further. I want to give the world a
          safe alternative to Dyrette; an AI
          that simply performs its function
          of protecting the internet from
          hackers.

                    BEN
          Yes!

                    INSPECTOR ERAS
          When you first arrived, you said
          you didn't care about anything
          anymore.

Mags smiles.

                    MAGS
          An AI that works for the benefit of
          the people, not profit.

                    INSPECTOR ERAS
          Israel could provide a starting
          place for you.

Mags smiles.

                    EMILY
          Mags, are you sure?

Mags rises and pulls Emily out into the hallway.

                    MAGS
          Excuse us.

                    BEN
          Emily. Jeez.

INT. ISRAELI INTELLIGENCE HQ - HALLWAY - NIGHT

Mags speaks in a hushed tone with Emily.

                    MAGS
          Emily, what are you doing?

                    EMILY
          He's a spy!

                    MAGS
          Of course, he is. So what? We're on
          his side now.

                    EMILY
          You are about to give him your
          technology! Are you sure?

                    MAGS
          Emily, you and I have been friends
          for a long time, right? If I want
          to do this, I will. You know that.
               (beat)
          Any enemy of my uncle is my friend.

Mags and Emily return to the Conference room.

INT. ISRAELI INTELLIGENCE HQ - CONFERENCE ROOM - NIGHT

Mags and Emily sit back down at the table. Ben and Inspector
Eras look at them with concern.

                    INSPECTOR ERAS
          Everything OK?

They nod.

Inspector Eras waves to a waiter, who brings over coffee.

                    BEN
          Tell us more about this Josephus
          guy.

INT. ROME - COUNTY ESTATE OF JOSEPHUS - GARDEN ROOM - DAY

Old Josephus continues to write in his diary and talk to
himself.

                    JOSEPHUS
          Some thought my conspiracy with the
          Romans was revenge against the
          Sanhedrin for appointing another
          general to replace me. Others
          thought it was to try to save my
          own skin. Still others said it was
          because I wanted to align myself
          with the fate of Vespasian--whom I
          knew would become a great Emperor.
          But I will tell you the real
          reason, my true motivation.

INT. ISRAELI INTELLIGENCE HQ - CONFERENCE ROOM - NIGHT

Ben and Emily are sipping their cups of coffee. Mags turns to
Inspector Eras.

                    MAGS
          Why do you think Josephus helped
          the Romans?

                    INSPECTOR ERAS
          My guess is he was hedging his
          bets.

                    MAGS
          I see.

                    INSPECTOR ERAS
          Josephus probably wasn't sure this
          Messiah, if he did come and
          conquer, would also get rid of what
          he regarded as Israel's internal
          enemy, the Sanhedrin priests. So,
          he plotted to get the Romans to
          extinguish them for him.

                    MAGS
          How?

                    INSPECTOR ERAS
          By conspiring with them to deprive
          the Sanhedrin priests of the seat
          of their power.

                    EMILY
          And what was that? Their temple?

                    INSPECTOR ERAS
          Very good, Emily. The Temple in
          Jerusalem. Josephus intended to get
          the Romans to strip the temple of
          its religious objects. Shall we?

                    EMILY
             (to Ben)
          Lots of things get stripped.

They rise and head into the hallway.

INT. ISRAELI INTELLIGENCE HQ - ADJACENT HALLWAY

Ben, Emily, and Mags follow Inspector Eras down the hall.

                    BEN
          Why would stripping the temple do
          that?

                    INSPECTOR ERAS
          The Temple was the center of the
          Jewish religion. For over a
          thousand years, the Jewish people
          had come to the Temple each year to
          make sacrifices for their sins.

                    MAGS
          I see. Take away temple sacrifice
          and you take away the soul of
          Jerusalem.

EXT. JERUSALEM - SKYLINE

SUPERIMPOSE: 70 A.D.

INT. JERUSALEM - HEZEKIAH'S TUNNEL - DAY

SUPERIMPOSE: JERUSALEM - HEZEKIAH'S TUNNEL

Josephus creeps into Fort Antonia through Hezekiah's tunnel,
wading through the water channel that's carved out of
limestone. He enters at a discreet location inside the fort.

INT. JERUSALEM - VESPASIAN'S LIVING QUARTERS - DAY

Josephus sneaks through Vespasian's living quarters, snuffing
out guards as he goes. Then he finds Vespasian in his
luxurious bathroom on his toilet. Josephus holds a knife to
his throat and hands him a wipe.

                    VESPASIAN
          What is it? Two years since we last
          saw each other in Nero's court?

                    JOSEPHUS
          Three.

                    VESPASIAN
          Nice to finally confront the
          general whose been stalling the
          progress of my armies in the north.
          Although I'd prefer different
          circumstances.

Josephus holds the knife closer. Vespasian wipes himself.

                         JOSEPHUS
          You want the Jews to submit to the
          will of Rome, I can show you how.

                         VESPASIAN
          Why will you help the Romans, Jew?

                         JOSEPHUS
          I have had a vision about your
          future.

INT. HAYWARD ENTERPRISES - CONTROL ROOM - DAY

The staff has left. Hayward paces alone in front of the map
on the video screen. Only Israel is red on the map. He
extends a hand and points a finger like a gun at the map.

                         HAYWARD
              Israel. O, Israel.

INT. JERUSALEM - ROMAN GUEST HOUSE - DAY

Luxurious guest house decorated in distinctive Roman style.
Josephus, wearing a new, expensive Roman toga, is in his
suite of rooms with windows overlooking the city skyline. He
paces on the terrace and then pauses to take in the view.

Second Temple is off in the distance. Josephus looks down at
his toga. He paces. He looks down again unsettled. He reaches
for the phylactery.

                         JOSEPHUS
                    (under his breath)
              Mother gave me this...

His eyes then narrow, focusing on the distant temple.

                         JOSEPHUS (CONT'D)
              Israel. O, Israel.

INT. HAYWARD ENTERPRISES - LOBBY - DAY

Brandon enters and surveys the lobby. He strolls confidently
over to the welcome desk which doubles as a security
checkpoint for the building.

A PHOTO behind the welcome desk on the wall reads: "RICHARD
HAYWARD."

                         BRANDON
              I need to see that guy. What floor?

The SECURITY GUARD lifts a phone receiver.

                    SECURITY GUARD
          Got an appointment?

                    BRANDON
          Nope. Just want to ask him a
          question.

                    SECURITY GUARD
               (snippy)
          I see. I don't believe he is in his
          office just now anyway; not that
          he'd even see you.
               (beat)
          Got ID?

Brandon walks away. As he's leaving, he sees a kiosk with
flyers. He takes one. He pauses to read.

The flyer reads: "BENEFIT FUND-RAISER CONCERT TONIGHT FOR
CARPAL TUNNEL SYNDROME"

A photo of Hayward conducting on orchestra appears on the
flyer.

EXT. SEA OF GALILEE - RESTAURANT - DAY

Humble seaside restaurant, updated. Modern fisherman sit
nearby eating. Inspector Eras, Mags, Ben, and Emily are
having lunch. They each have an English transcript of
Josephus's Diary. Emily looks up from the transcript.

                    EMILY
          I guess ancient people faced
          challenges, too.

Everyone nods as though it's obvious.

EXT. RESIDENTIAL AREA OF JERUSALEM - JOSEPHUS' PARENTS HOME -
DAY

SUPERIMPOSE: OUTSKIRTS OF JERUSALEM

Dressed plainly, Josephus walks slowly up the path to his
parents' doorway. He hesitates then enters.

INT. JOSEPHUS' PARENTS' HOME - DAY

Josephus meets his MOTHER just inside the doorway. They hug.
His younger sister, LOGAN (14) joyfully greets him.

                    MOTHER
          So glad you're safe, my son!

                    JOSEPHUS
          It's not going well with the
          Romans.

They move into the kitchen area. Logan watches on adoringly.

                    MOTHER
          It wasn't going well with the
          Seleucids either 200 years ago.

                    JOSEPHUS
          These are Romans, mother, not
          Greeks. Israel is a minor
          irritation for them.

                    MOTHER
          You are fulfilling the Almighty's
          work for you, my child.

                    JOSEPHUS
          So you've told me since I was a
          boy.

                    MOTHER
          Just like the Maccabees, you will
          defeat them. I'm sure of it.

Josephus' FATHER comes in. They great each other warmly.

                    FATHER
          And remember, son, after they
          entered Jerusalem, the first thing
          they did was re-establish temple
          sacrifice.

                    MOTHER
          Our own relative, Jonathan
          Maccabee, named high priest!

                    JOSEPHUS
          I won't forget.

                    FATHER
          Walk with me.

EXT. JOSEPHUS' PARENTS' HOME - GARDEN AREA - DAY

The Father and Josephus walk into the garden area of the
enclosure.

                    FATHER
          You worry me with your tolerance of
          our Jewish brethren who embrace the
          Greek ways; these Hellenizers.

                    JOSEPHUS
          Please don't expect from me the
          same as you do yourself. I am not a
          rabbi.

                    FATHER
          Is it so hard to savor our rich
          history, son? Maccabees aside, our
          tradition goes back a thousand
          years or more!

                    JOSEPHUS
          Not hard, father.

The Father beckons Josephus to have a seat. A kind of
rabbinic catechism follows.

                    FATHER
          Abraham who established our nation.

                    JOSEPHUS
          The famine that led his grandson
          Jacob into Egypt.

                    FATHER
          Our escape from Pharaoh and return
          to the promised land under Joshua.

                    JOSEPHUS
               (wryly)
          After 40 years of wandering with
          Moses.

                    FATHER
          The majesty of David.

                    JOSEPHUS
          And his scandal with Bathsheba.

                    FATHER
          Solomon and the glory of his
          Temple!

                    JOSEPHUS
          Our fall into captivity in Babylon.

                    FATHER
          Nehemiah's rebuilding of the walls
          of Jerusalem.

                         JOSEPHUS
          And then came our forebears the
          Maccabees, of course.

                         FATHER
          I have taught you well. Our faith
          is what's most important. And how
          do we show that best...?

                         JOSEPHUS
          ...in our religious practices.

                         FATHER
          Temple sacrifice; a lamb offered
          for a person's sins.

                         JOSEPHUS
          Father, what of messiah? I know so
          little.

                         FATHER
          How do you mean?

                         JOSEPHUS
          A conqueror? A martyr? This passage
          from Isaiah vexes me...
               (beat)
          With his stripes we are healed.

                         FATHER
          A king from David's line, who will
          rule us during the world to come.
               (beat)
          Surely, our Messiah wouldn't
          sacrifice himself.

INT. JOSEPHUS' PARENTS' HOME - DAY

Josephus and his Father return to the kitchen area. Josephus
hugs his sister Logan goodbye.

                         MOTHER
          Won't you stay with us for Seder?

Josephus presses the phylactery into his mother's hand. He
hugs both his parents and exits.

INT. JERUSALEM - ROMAN GUEST HOUSE - DAY

Josephus is dressing. A SERVANT stands by. A Roman toga and a
Jewish aristocrat's robe are laid out before him.

He ponders. Then, he dons the Jewish robe. He beckons the servant to hold a reflecting glass before him. He observes...

EXT. JERUSALEM - WEST OF THE OLD CITY WALLS - DAY

SUPERIMPOSE: JAFFA GATE - ROMAN SIEGE

Titus and Josephus are on horseback, galloping around the base of the inner-city wall. TIBERIAS (24), second in command, accompanies them. Roman soldiers are constructing an outer wall and ramparts.

                    TIBERIAS
          That wall will serve to starve out
          the city. And the ramparts our
          soldiers are constructing will
          cross over into the city.

They slow to a walk. Hebrew soldiers and politicians look down from atop the inner wall.

                    TIBERIAS (CONT'D)
          I can summon more soldiers to
          accompany us, Prefect. At your
          command.

                    TITUS
          Not necessary, as we've discussed.

                    JOSEPHUS
          Indeed, Prefect.

Josephus holds up the banner of peace to buttress his comment.

The three generals stop at the Jaffa Gate. Titus raps on it.

Slowly, a door in the gate opens and two JEWISH EMISSARIES emerge.

Josephus and Tiberias dismount and walk to greet them. A conversation begins. At that moment, an arrow hits Tiberias in the shoulder blade. He goes down.

Simultaneously, two JEWISH ASSASSINS in disguise outside the wall throw back their hoods and grab Titus off his horse. They attempt to drag him to the door in the gate.

Josephus intercepts them and single-handedly fights off the assassins. Roman soldiers belatedly arrive to help. He attempts to move Titus off to safety. Titus stands on his own and refuses. Titus then straightens his breastplate and walks off. He scowls blame at his soldiers and Josephus.

Josephus then helps Tiberias. Tiberias is bewildered at
Titus' demeanor.

INT. MILITARY FORTRESS ANTONIA - MILITARY PLANNING ROOM - DAY

Vespasian, Josephus, Titus, a bandaged Tiberias and a
GENERAL (50s) gather around a large map of Jerusalem on a
table. Josephus is wearing his new Roman toga. He uses a
pointing stick as he speaks.

                    JOSEPHUS
          In the evening, the temple guard
          changes. This will be your
          opportunity to enter with a minimum
          of resistance.

                    VESPASIAN
          You are certain our confiscation of
          the temple implements will be
          sufficient?

                    JOSEPHUS
          That is all that is necessary.

                    TITUS
          No blood? No destruction? I find it
          hard to believe.

                    VESPASIAN
          Titus, why use the sword when a
          creative accusation will do?
               (beat)
          Jupiter knows your methods have
          proven ineffective thus far.

Titus glares at Josephus.

                    JOSEPHUS
          Then on to the Sanhedrin. Arrest
          them all.

                    TITUS
          More accusations? Truly?

Just then, a MESSENGER enters. He hands the message to
Vespasian then backs away. Vespasian reads it.

                    VESPASIAN
          It seems young Josephus's vision
          about me has come true. I am called
          to Rome.

All congratulate Vespasian. Vespasian beckons Josephus. They
prepare to leave the room together. Titus casts a jealous
eye. Vespasian looks back.

                    VESPASIAN (CONT'D)
          Titus will lead you.
               (beat)
          Step it up, son.

They leave.

                    TITUS
          I have other plans. The Jews are no
          friends of Rome.

INT. ISRAELI INTELLIGENCE HQ - TYPICAL OFFICE - DAY

Mags is coding. She stops suddenly and confronts Emily.

                    MAGS
          What were you thinking, calling my
          stepmother?

                    EMILY
          I was worried about you!

                    MAGS
          I can take care of myself.

Ben gets up, hovers over her and studies the screen.

                    BEN
          If you'd like any assistance, just
          say the word...

Mags smiles sweetly and shakes her head. Ben sits down.

                    EMILY
               (to Ben)
          Like you are going to give her
          coding advice?

                    BEN
          I think humans are going to evolve
          a sixth finger on each hand
          someday.

                    EMILY
          That's stupid.

                    BEN
          No, it is not. It will be for the
          space bar.
               (MORE)

                    BEN (CONT'D)
          Studies show the time it takes
          between hitting the space bar and
          another key is the longest of all
          the keys. It's only evolution.

                    EMILY
          If Brandon were here, he'd say it's
          stupid, too.

                    BEN
          Mags, what do you think?

Mags smiles sweetly. Emily casts a jealous eye.

                    MAGS
          I think it's the question mark.

EXT. POOR SUBURB OF MAJOR CITY - NIGHT

Brandon drives his motorcycle through a depressed
neighborhood. He passes poorly kept cookie cutter housing and
an old-fashioned strip shopping center with vacant units.
Homeless people hang around on street corners.

Brandon turns down a street and into the driveway of one of
these small homes. He does not rev the motor. He removes his
helmet and uses the kickstand.

He walks up the front stoop, kicking debris off it as he goes
and pulls open the broken screen door. He enters.

INT. BRANDON'S OLD FAMILY HOME - FRONT ROOM - NIGHT

A TV is blaring in the front room. Brandon's UNCLE JOHN (60)
dozes on a beat-up old couch before it.

                    BRANDON
          Hey, Uncle John.

Uncle John wakes up and waves to Brandon as he struggles to
get up to greet him. He accidentally knocks over an empty
bottle of beer.

                    BRANDON (CONT'D)
          Dad's old gun still here?

Uncle John struggles to remember. Then nods and beckons him.
Brandon follows him into the bedroom.

INT. BRANDON'S OLD FAMILY HOME - BEDROOM - NIGHT

Brandon watches as Uncle John pulls the old gun out of a drawer.

                    BRANDON
          Show me how to us it?

                    UNCLE JOHN
          What's it for?

                    BRANDON
          Protection.

                    UNCLE JOHN
          What am I gonna use?

                    BRANDON
          I'll bring it back.

Uncle John ponders then nods.

                    UNCLE JOHN
          I guess it's yours anyway.

Uncle John then loads several bullets, aims it, and mimics pulling the trigger.

                    UNCLE JOHN (CONT'D)
          Simple, huh?

Brandon nods. He takes out the bullets. Puts the gun and bullets in his backpack.

                    UNCLE JOHN (CONT'D)
          You need to kill somebody, hold the
          barrel to their forehead and
          squeeze.

Brandon looks startled for a moment, then nods.

                    BRANDON
          I guess.
               (beat)
          Thanks, Uncle John.

INT. ISRAELI INTELLIGENCE HQ - OFFICE - DAY

Inspector Eras bursts in, interrupting Emily and Mags.

                    INSPECTOR ERAS
          Time is short.

                         MAGS
               Have to start from scratch.

Inspector Eras beckons an Agent ARIEL. He nods to him. Agent
Ariel exits and returns, wheeling Mags' server on a rack.

                         MAGS (CONT'D)
               You took it?

                         EMILY
               You let us think Mags' uncle
               burglarized us?
                    (to Mags)
               Mags, he's got your technology.

Mags holds down the delete key, rapidly erasing lines of
code.

A horrified look crosses Inspector Eras's face.

                         MAGS
               How am I supposed to trust you?! My
               uncle, now you?

Mags storms out.

                         EMILY
                    (to Ben)
               I told you he's a spy.

                         BEN
                    (to AGENT ARIEL)
               That's how you knew to find us at
               the airport. You spied on us!

Inspector Eras and Agent ARIEL exchange a look.

Ben and Emily run after her but are too late. Mags leaves the
facility through an emergency exit door and emerges into a
desert.

EXT. DEAD SEA AREA - DESERT - DAY

Mags squints in the sun. Its blazing hot. She groans
realizing she's here again. Stony cliffs. Rocks and scrub
vegetation. Dead Sea off in the distance. Mags stands
dumbfounded. No one and nothing nearby.

INT. HAYWARD ENTERPRISES - CONTROL ROOM - NIGHT

Technician is in the process of establishing a video link on
a large projection screen with the Knesset in Jerusalem.

Larry and Geoffrey stand by. Hayward on the phone with
Israel's KNESSET PRIME MINISTER (60's), a man with dark
eyebrows under a shock of white hair.

                    HAYWARD
          Deliver Israel to me. I'll let you
          stay in office.

INT. KNESSET - DAY

On the floor of the Knesset between sessions members are
milling about, talking in groups.

On the phone-

                    KNESSET PRIME MINISTER
          Yes, Mr. Hayward. You have a deal.

Knesset Prime Minister notices the MESSIANIC COALITION LEADER
(60s) chatting nearby with other members. They exchange a
look. Knesset Prime Minister wipes the sweat from above his
lip. Messianic Coalition Leader narrows his eyes at him
giving him a suspicious look.

A LEGISLATIVE ASSISTANT comes up to the Knesset Prime
Minister.

                    LEGISLATIVE ASSISTANT
          Issues with the Messianic
          Coalition?

                    KNESSET PRIME MINISTER
          Always.

EXT. DEAD SEA AREA - DESERT - DAY

Mags walks alone in the desert. She notices a fissure in a
cliff. She enters.

INT. CLIFFS BY THE DEAD SEA - ESSENE RUINS - DAY

Mags looks around. She discovers it is an ancient habitat of
some sort; a community meeting room. Suddenly, she
experiences a...

DOUBLE EXPOSURE-LIKE OVERLAY: ESSENE MEETING CHAMBER 59 A.D.

Monk One and Monk Two, as their younger selves, stand before
the Essene tribunal panel. Earlier scene re-enacted.

Inspector Eras enters from a hidden interior door in the
chamber. He doesn't see the overlay but only the ruins. He
quietly watches her. She watches the overlay with
fascination.

                    INSPECTOR ERAS
          The two Essene monks we discussed?
          My ancestors, one by blood I think,
          and both by religious legacy.

Mags moves closer to the images of the monks. She stares
transfixed.

                    INSPECTOR ERAS (CONT'D)
          Here in these ruins long ago, we
          believe. We have kept alive their
          hope of a twice-appearing messiah
          throughout our generations. My
          father and his father and so on…

Double exposure-like overlay fades.

INT. JERUSALEM - KNESSET - DAY

A video link is being established with Hayward Enterprises
Control Room. Hayward comes into view on a large screen. He
is chuckling. The Technician, Larry, and Geoffrey step into
view on screen and glare back at the Knesset members.

                    HAYWARD (ON SCREEN)
          You think you can do without the
          Dyrette? You are mistaken. Welcome
          my wafers. Welcome me! I am your
          savior. You have 1 hour.

INT. CLIFFS BY THE DEAD SEA - ESSENE RUINS - DAY

Mags narrows her eyes at Inspector Eras, giving him an angry
look.

                    INSPECTOR ERAS
          Now you know our story. I'm sorry I
          didn't tell you earlier about the
          server. Our desperation, you see.

He moves closer to Mags. Holds up plane tickets.

                    INSPECTOR ERAS (CONT'D)
          I have three plane tickets for you
          if you wish to leave. I won't stop
          you.

Mags softens.

                    MAGS
          I see now the story is much richer.

                    INSPECTOR ERAS
          Indeed, it is.

                    MAGS
          My friend Brandon once told me
          there's no reason... really... for
          freedom from Dyrette's supervision
          or any other kind of despotism, for
          that matter, unless you truly
          believe there is meaning to our
          lives.

                    INSPECTOR ERAS
               (nodding)
          Will you help us now?

                    MAGS
          A twice appearing messiah. I guess
          when you hope for something really
          important, you do what it takes.

Inspector Eras then pulls out a remote control and presses a
button. A large door at the rear of the Essene chamber ruins
opens, revealing a state-of-the-art coding room with numerous
workstations manned with coders.

INT. HAYWARD ENTERPRISES - CONTROL ROOM - NIGHT

Hayward paces while staring at the clock. Time ticks.

INT. CLIFFS BY THE DEAD SEA - ESSENE RUINS - CODING ROOM -
DAY

Inspector Eras and Mags walk to what has been designated
Mags's workstation. Her server is on a rack nearby. Ben and
Emily enter apprehensively from a side door nearby. Mags
gives them a reassuring smile.

                    INSPECTOR ERAS
          My coders are ready to assist you
          with activating your system on
          Israel's internet.

Mags begins hooking up the server and adjusting the settings.
Inspector Eras eyes the server.

                    MAGS
          It creates high velocity randomized
          spoofing protocols which will hide
          Israel from hackers while the AI is
          doing its learning thing. Hackers
          can't hack because they can't see
          and therefore target your
          industries and communication.

                    INSPECTOR ERAS
          Cloaked then?

                    MAGS
               (under her breath)
          We'll find out.

Agent Ariel brings a cell phone to Inspector Eras. He takes
the call.

INT. KNESSET - DAY

INTERCUT: Knesset and Coding Room.

On the phone-

                    MESSIANIC COALITION LEADER
          Our hopes and prayers are with you.

Inspector Eras nods, then gravely ends the call.

INT. CLIFFS BY THE DEAD SEA - ESSENE RUINS - CODING ROOM -
DAY

Mags finishes hooking up her server. She coordinates with the
local coders assisting her, then turns to ONE OF THE CODERS.

                    MAGS
          Ready?

One Of The Coders nods. Inspector Eras looks at his watch.

                    MAGS (CONT'D)
               (to Inspector Eras)
          Is there time to test it?

Inspector Eras shakes his head, "no." Mags flips the
activation switch. A warning alarm is heard.

                    EMILY
               (matter of factly)
          It's down.

Everyone looks at the server. It's flashing. Dead silence.
Mags looks, paralyzed.

Emily exchanges a long skeptical look with Inspector Eras and
then nods to Ben. Ben placidly walks over and whacks the
server on its side. The flashing stops.

INT. HAYWARD ENTERPRISES - CONTROL ROOM - NIGHT

Hayward looks at his watch and nods to the Technician.

                    TECHNICIAN
          Disable Dyrette?

                    HAYWARD
          Let's feed them to the hackers!

The Technician codes. Hayward watches his video screen
greedily.

ON VIDEO SCREEN

It's downtown Jerusalem during rush hour. Nothing unusual is
happening. Cars are sitting in traffic. There's no evidence
of dystopia.

BACK TO SCENE

The Technician checks and rechecks the settings. Hayward
looks furious! He beckons Larry and Geoffrey.

                    HAYWARD
          Did you ever find Mags' server?

                    LARRY
          No, boss.

Frustrated, Hayward pounds a nearby desk with his fist and
runs his hands through his hair, messing it up.

INT. CLIFFS BY THE DEAD SEA - ESSENE RUINS - CODING ROOM -
DAY

Inspector Eras takes a phone call and smiles. He points to a
large video screen.

ON VIDEO SCREEN

There's no dystopia in downtown Jerusalem during rush hour.
The cars slowly cross the intersection. Life goes on as
usual.

INT. CLIFFS BY THE DEAD SEA - ESSENE RUINS - CODING ROOM -
DAY

Cheers erupt in the room. Senior coders gather around Mags.
Lesser technicians gather around Ben. Inspector Eras and Mags
exchange a knowing look of approval for her efforts. Emily
breaks into a smile for Ben.

Inspector Eras beckons Mags, Ben and Emily into a small
unfurnished room adjoining the Essene Coding Chamber.

                    INSPECTOR ERAS
          A three-way video link has been
          established for us.

INT. SMALL ROOM ADJOINING THE ESSENE CODING CHAMBER - DAY

Inspector Eras and Mags watch the screen. Ben and Emily stand
behind them, observing the screen.

ON VIDEO SCREEN

INTERCUT: HAYWARD ENTERPRISES, KNESSET, AND SMALL ROOM

Knesset members are cheering and celebrating. Hayward's hair
is still messed up. Messianic Coalition Leader smiling.

Hayward glares at the Knesset Prime Minister and pulls his
finger menacingly across his throat. Hayward then interrupts
the cheering politicians.

                    HAYWARD
          Israel, you are a tiny country. You
          are nothing on the world stage!
          And, you have the arrogance to set
          up your own protocol.

Laughter, then boos from the Knesset members.

                    HAYWARD (CONT'D)
          There is only one person who can
          design a system like Dyrette. And
          that is my niece.

Silence falls.

                    HAYWARD (CONT'D)
          So, ...you must have her. You've
          taken something that belongs to me.
                    (shouting)
          From me!

Mags steps into view of the camera.

                    MAGS
          Thank you, Uncle. Nice to finally
          get credit.

Cheers erupt from the Knesset members. A round of applause.

                    HAYWARD
          Mags, dear. Obviously, they've
          brainwashed you.

Silence falls.

                    HAYWARD (CONT'D)
               (to Mags)
          And, they have forced you to work
          for them! Poor girl.

Titters of incredulity.

                    HAYWARD (CONT'D)
          But, we're family, Mags. I promise
          to rescue you no matter what
          they've done to you. ...even if I
          have to send the world to find you.
               (beat)
          And Israel will be mine!

Mags points at his head.

                    MAGS
          Hmm. Your hair?

Hayward self-consciously smooths his hair The video link
terminates.

More cheers!

EXT. DEAD SEA RESORT - DAY

Ben, Emily, Inspector Eras, and Mags are floating on their
backs in the Dead Sea at the resort's luxurious beach.

An Israeli Jet fighter roars down the mid point of the Dead
Sea on patrol. A sonic boom erupts overhead as it passes by
the resort. It draws their attention momentarily.

They resume relaxing. Ben is holding a gaudy cocktail and
taking sips. The Sea is only a few feet deep. They are
unusually buoyant and awkward in the salty water but amused
with the phenomena.

                    BEN
          I wonder what your uncle means,
          "even if I have to send the world
          to find you?"

As the realization hits, they struggle to their feet. Emily
strokes the cross on her necklace.

                    EMILY
          Not thinking that means he wants to
          come floating with us.

                    INSPECTOR ERAS
          Jerusalem is alone, it seems.

                    MAGS
          The world versus us?

INT. HAYWARD ENTERPRISES - CONTROL ROOM - NIGHT

Hayward still self-consciously smooths back his hair.

                    HAYWARD
               (to Geoffrey)
          The Jews have fueled her ambition.
               (to all employees in
                earshot)
          Come! Come here. Now!

With a furious look, Hayward summons Larry, Geoffrey, and the
Technician. They line up and stand before him like mute
soldiers. Numerous other employees soon gather behind them to
listen.

EXT. MILITARY FORTRESS ANTONIA - PARADE GROUNDS - 70 A.D. -
DAY

A horn summoning solders is blown.

Roman army is methodically mustering. They line up before
Titus who is on a horse. Josephus and other generals flank
Titus on horses. Titus turns to a GENERAL.

                    TITUS
               (quietly to the General
                regarding Josephus)
          My father has fueled his ambition.

The mustering continues.

INT. HAYWARD ENTERPRISES - CONTROL ROOM - NIGHT

Hayward steps forward to address his employees, looking
piercingly into the faces of his employees as he speaks.

                    HAYWARD
          My loyal employees. We have shown
          the world, country by country, why
          it is in their interest to adopt my
          wafer technology.

Employees affirm him. Hayward points at the map.

                    HAYWARD (CONT'D)
          Israel is the lone holdout. It has
          chosen to employ its own protocol
          with the help of my niece.

Larry steps forward and pumps his fist in the air.

                    LARRY
               (trying to build support)
          Traitor, traitor!

Hayward sees nods of support from the audience. A patronizing
grin appears on Hayward's face.

                    HAYWARD
          If we can't convince Israel to join
          us the way we have convinced the
          others, we shall have to use a
          different means of persuasion.

                    GEOFFREY
               (inviting participation)
          Tell us. Tell us!

                    HAYWARD
          We shall provoke the very world
          itself against Israel!

Hayward steps out of view. A curtain opens at one end of the
control room, revealing a large auditorium and stage.

A cascade of "oohs and aahs" come from the audience.

INT. HAYWARD ENTERPRISES - STAGE - DAY

Four computer workstations are arranged in a semi-circle
facing a huge screen at the back of the stage.

Hayward's employees now find seats in the auditorium. Other
employees file in from entrance doors.

Hayward walks out from the wing of the stage like he is a
symphony conductor. Massive cheering erupts from his staff.
He steps onto a podium at the apex of the semicircle facing
the audience.

                    HAYWARD
          Let me introduce to you to the
          world's finest hackers!

                    GEOFFREY
              (confides to Larry)
          Boss may have just changed the
          rules.

Four hackers wait in the wings, all in their 20's. Hayward
introduces them, one by one, THE CONQUEROR, THE INSTIGATOR,
THE CENTRAL BANKER, and THE GRIM REAPER. Each wears a
signature color of white, red, black, or pale.

                    HAYWARD
          The Conqueror, The Instigator, The
          Central Banker, and The Grim
          Reaper.

As he does so, each one respectively takes his or her seat at
one of the four workstations as though he or she was
preparing to play an instrument. Hayward lifts his baton in
readiness to conduct a "hacking symphony."

EXT. MILITARY FORTRESS ANTONIA - PARADE GROUNDS - 70 A.D. -
DAY

Solders continue to muster.

With a stern look, Titus turns to his General and Josephus.

                    TITUS
          You two do reconnaissance. We'll
          join you at the Temple.

Josephus and the General ride off on their horses.

The solders finish mustering and fall silent.

Titus nods to his QUARTERMASTER, who then blows a whistle.

From storage buildings around the parade grounds; battering
rams, demolition machines, siege engines, carts, axes, ropes,
and hammers emerge and are mustered for the march to the
temple. Soldiers gird themselves with swords and shields for
an assault.

Titus lifts his baton of authority and is met with cheers.

INT. HAYWARD ENTERPRISES - STAGE - NIGHT

With his baton, Hayward points and directs the audience's
attention to the video screen.

                    HAYWARD
          Behold, a prelude!

BEGIN VIDEO SEQUENCE:

EXT. MAJOR CITY - DAY

SUPERIMPOSE: PRESENT DAY

Survey of blighted urban area with high density housing and
industrial mix.

EXT. SMALL TRACT HOUSE - DAY

A MIDDLE-AGED GRANDFATHER uses a push mower over his tiny
lawn. He wears a wife beater and smokes. He limps decidedly.

INT. SMALL TRACT HOUSE - DAY

Living room congested with worn out furniture. A MIDDLE-AGED
GRANDMOTHER in a ripped house dress leans over and comforts
an INFANT who is crying in a bassinet. A TV blares a game
show nearby.

As she comforts the baby, the MOTHER and FATHER of the infant
come in. It's apparent Mother has been crying. Father sadly
shows Grandmother a pink slip. Grandmother beckons Father and
Mother over. They all gather around the bassinet and smile at
the sleeping infant's contentment.

EXT. BANK - ATM STATION - DAY

WORKING-CLASS MAN collects money as it spits out of the ATM
machine. A little more comes out than he expects. When it is
finished, he pockets the money and strolls happily down the
street to a neighborhood bar. He enters it.

INT. BAR - DAY

Working-Class Man enters to see his CO-WORKERS already at the
bar. They cheerfully greet him. He joins them. They pat him
on the back. He sips a cheap beer.

EXT. URBAN PARK AND PICNIC AREA - DAY

A WORKING CLASS FAMILY is ferrying a junk food picnic from
their late model station wagon to a picnic table. The park is
in poor repair with overflowing trash bins but congested with
an AMALGAM OF PEOPLE recreating and relaxing.

EXT. MAIN STREET - DAY

Run-down urban shopping area. Several stores closed. KIDS
riding on skate boards. A tattooed TEEN BOY walks with a
tattooed TEEN GIRL holding hands. The girl is smoking.

Teen Girl looks at her cell phone. She shows it to the Teen
Boy. They beckon nearby FRIENDS. All look at their cell
phones. Teen Boy points in the opposite directing they were
walking. All walk decidedly in that direction.

Off in the distance is a railroad track crossing.

EXT. RAILROAD TRACKS - DAY

Also walking towards the railroad tracks from different
directions are the rest of the characters in this sequence.
They begin to join up.

(Consider "Working Class Hero" by Marianne Faithfull)

MANY OTHERS like them join them as well. They arrive en masse
at a train track crossing opposite a wealthy area of the
city. They carry sledge hammers, push empty shopping carts,
hoes, etc. Middle Aged Grandfather pushes his mower as a
weapon. Together they form the MASSES.

As they walk and gather momentum, a SPEECH MAKER (30s) rouses
the crowd.

                    SPEECH MAKER
          If nothing else, all of human
          history teaches us one thing; the
          rich have always oppressed the
          poor. We must not allow ourselves
          to suffer. It's time...

The Masses raucously whistle and affirm the Speech Maker.

                    SPEECH MAKER (CONT'D)
          And we, the working poor of this
          age, find ourselves begging the
          scraps given to us by the
          governments and the businesses the
          rich control.

More jeering and affirmations come from the Masses.

                         SPEECH MAKER (CONT'D)
               Those who own the means of
               production, including the tech
               industry which now dominates our
               world, have for too long exploited
               us.
                    (beat)
               And now the time is upon us to
               fight back! Let the many who have
               nothing take back from the few who
               have all! Rise up I say! Go and
               crush them! You are the Conquerors!

          MASSES   SPEECH MAKER (CONT'D)
        (in unison)   (in unison)
     Conquerors!   Conquerors!

The Masses arrive at the train tracks and stop. Silence
falls.

END VIDEO SEQUENCE.

INT. HAYWARD ENTERPRISES - STAGE - NIGHT

A sinister grin crosses Hayward's face as watches the end of
the video sequence. Silent anticipation fills the room. He
lifts his baton in readiness.

SUPERIMPOSE: THE CONQUEROR'S SONATA

SUPERIMPOSE: THERE BEFORE ME WAS A WHITE HORSE! ITS RIDER
HELD A BOW, AND HE WAS GIVEN A CROWN, AND HE RODE OUT AS A
CONQUEROR BENT ON CONQUEST.

Hayward directs his baton at The Conqueror. The Conqueror
starts coding.

                         AUDIENCE
                    (chants louder in unison)
               A noble, global peasant revolt. A
               noble, global peasant revolt.

ON VIDEO SCREEN

"PERIMETER COMPROMISED" appears as a flashing text across the
screen.

Text lines begin to appear sequentially on the screen:

--PRIVATE SECURITY SYSTEMS NOW DISABLED

--COMMUNICATIONS JAMMED

--ELECTRONIC DOORS UNLOCKED

--POLICE VEHICLES HOBBLED

--PHONE SERVICE INTERRUPTED

--FIREARMS OFFLINE.

Then, a series of error codes appear on the screen in the following order:

--ERROR CODE 404

--ERROR CODE 500

--ERROR CODE 401

INT./EXT. WEALTHY AREA OF THE CITY - DAY

With a great roar, the Masses pour over the train tracks into the wealthy area. Barricades erected by security guards greet the Masses as they enter.

The Masses over-run the barricades and guards who have disabled weapons. They run first to a luxurious country club/marina complex with fancy restaurants and a high-end shopping district. Rampant destruction ensues.

EXT. JERUSALEM - 70 A.D. - NIGHT

SUPERIMPOSE: JERUSALEM 70 A.D.

Roman soldiers march through the city, disrupting local activity as they go. They push over vendors' carts, trample the disabled, send children running, and loot fruit.

Roman soldiers reach the Temple mount. They file into the temple.

Josephus and Titus enter with them.

INT. TEMPLE - NIGHT

Josephus watches as the soldiers confiscate the religious artifacts over the objections of the priests. Among the artifacts used in worship are candlesticks, tongs, etc.

ONE PRIEST steps forward to obstruct the soldiers' progress and is pushed to the ground violently by a MENACING SOLDIER.

Then the CHIEF PRIEST and his ENTOURAGE attempt to halt the progression. Menacing Soldier becomes enraged.

Josephus looks alarmed. He and Titus exchange looks.

> JOSEPHUS
> Titus, this is not necessary!

Titus nods to Menacing Soldier.

Menacing Soldier runs his short sword through the chest of the Chief Priest.

> MENACING SOLDIER
> (to Chief Priest)
> Off you go. You are no longer
> needed here.

The Menacing Soldier plunges the sword deeper into the Chief Priest and yanks it back out. He smiles as he watches the Chief Priest fall backwards on the ground.

Other priests come to his aid. MORE PRIESTS begin to fight back, but they get killed in the ensuing struggle.

Josephus watches on in horror and regret. Titus grins, then exits the Temple.

INT. HAYWARD ENTERPRISES - STAGE - NIGHT

Hayward draws the attention of the second coder. A hush falls.

SUPERIMPOSE: THE INSTIGATOR'S ADAGIO... THEN ANOTHER HORSE
             CAME OUT, A FIERY RED ONE. ITS RIDER WAS GIVEN
             POWER TO TAKE PEACE FROM THE EARTH AND TO MAKE
             PEOPLE KILL EACH OTHER. TO HIM WAS GIVEN A LARGE
             SWORD.

> HAYWARD
> Let's stir up some trouble for
> Israel, shall we?

Hayward lifts his baton and points at The Instigator. The Instigator begins to code, typing furiously on the keyboard.

Three similar scene sequences follow in rapid succession.

ON SCREEN

A map of the Middle East appears. No lines delineating countries and no labels. A video of a missile is being launched.

On the map, a tracking line originates somewhere far north of Israel. It travels to the Golan Heights, followed by an illustration of the explosion.

INT. NORTH OF ISRAEL - DAY

SUPERIMPOSE: UNDERGROUND MILITARY INSTALLATION NORTH OF
            ISRAEL

NORTHERN TECHNICIANS before missile control panels look confused and greatly alarmed. They are Russian born.

BACK TO SCENE

On stage, Hayward watches on approvingly.

                    HAYWARD
          They think they did it! Those fools
          haven't got a clue.

INT. KNESSET - FLOOR - DAY

Murmurs ripple around the room as the POLITICIANS are collaborating in earnest about the attack. The Knesset Prime Minister stands before the Knesset members, struggling to regain credibility.

                    KNESSET PRIME MINISTER
          The Northern Powers are clearly
          responsible for this attack. They
          must be held accountable. Save the
          Golan Heights!

                    KNESSET MEMBERS
          Meet force with equal force. Force
          with force!

INT. HAYWARD ENTERPRISES - STAGE - NIGHT

With a satisfied look on his face, Hayward watches the screen with great interest.

                    HAYWARD
          Wait for it.

ON SCREEN

A map of the Middle East appears again. No lines delineating countries and no labels. A missile is being launched. A tracking line originates in the Golan Heights.

It travels to where the missile was launched north of Israel, followed by an illustration of the explosion.

INT. NORTH OF ISRAEL - UNDERGROUND MILITARY INSTALLATION
NORTH OF ISRAEL - DAY

Explosion rocks the bunker, sending debris falling from the ceiling. Northern Technicians look shaken up. Some fall out of their chairs by the thunderous impact.

INT. HAYWARD ENTERPRISES - STAGE - NIGHT

Hayward laughs loudly. Cheers erupt from the audience. Using his baton, Hayward points at the screen.

                    HAYWARD
          More to come, my loyal employees.
          Watch the screen and enjoy the
          chaos. Now, you'll see how we get
          the world to do our dirty work.

ON SCREEN

A MOSCOW BORN LEADER appears, head of the Northern Powers. He sits astride his grand horse like Napoleon before his armies.

                    MOSCOW BORN LEADER
          We attack Israel!

EXT. NORTH OF ISRAEL - DAY

SUPERIMPOSE: STRONGHOLD OF THE NORTHERN POWERS

Northern Armies move out.

INT. HAYWARD ENTERPRISES - STAGE - NIGHT

Hayward lifts his baton and points again at The Instigator. The Instigator nods and begins to code, typing quickly.

ON SCREEN

A map of the Middle East appears. No lines delineating countries and no labels. A missile is being launched. A tracking line originates to the far east of Israel. It travels to Jerusalem, followed by an illustration of the explosion.

Hayward watches on with wild eyes, laughing with satisfaction.

                    HAYWARD
          Jerusalem got it this time! This
          ought to wake them up.

INT. EAST OF ISRAEL - UNDERGROUND MILITARY INSTALLATION EAST
OF ISRAEL - DAY

SUPERIMPOSE: UNDERGROUND MILITARY INSTALLATION EAST OF ISRAEL

EASTERN TECHNICIANS sitting before the missile control panels
look at each other with confusion. They are Chinese born.

INT. KNESSET - FLOOR - DAY

Panicked looks appear on the faces of the politicians as they
discuss among each other about the attack.

                    KNESSET MEMBERS
          An eye for an eye!

                    KNESSET PRIME MINISTER
                    (gaining confidence)
          The Eastern Powers must be held
          accountable for this action.

INT. HAYWARD ENTERPRISES - STAGE - NIGHT

Hayward is laughing.

ON SCREEN

A map of the Middle East appears. No lines delineating
countries and no labels. A missile is being launched. A
tracking line originates in Jerusalem. It travels to where
the second missile was launched east of Israel, followed by
an illustration of the explosion.

INT. UNDERGROUND MILITARY INSTALLATION EAST OF ISRAEL - DAY

Explosion rocks the bunker. The sheer force throws the
Eastern Technicians out of their seats. Huge chunks of
ceiling debris fall on them, crushing their arms and legs.

INT. HAYWARD ENTERPRISES - STAGE - NIGHT

Cheers erupt from Hayward's audience. Hayward smiles and
takes a bow, playing to their enthusiasm.

ON SCREEN

A BEIJING BORN LEADER appears. He sits astride his grand horse like a great Khan before his armies.

                    BEIJING BORN LEADER
          We attack Israel!

EXT. EAST OF ISRAEL - DAY

SUPERIMPOSE: STRONGHOLD OF THE EASTERN POWERS

Eastern Armies move out. It's a huge, "200 million man" army.

INT. HAYWARD ENTERPRISES - STAGE - NIGH

Boisterous applause fills the room. Hayward is bowing.

Hayward lifts his baton and points again at The Instigator. The Instigator nods. And with a grin on his face, he begins to code.

ON SCREEN

A map of the Middle East appears. No lines delineating countries and no labels. A missile is being launched. A tracking line originates to the far south of Israel. It travels to Tel Aviv on the map, followed by an illustration of the explosion.

BACK TO SCENE

Hayward watches on approvingly, then turns to his audience.

                    HAYWARD
          We're making history!

INT. UNDERGROUND MILITARY INSTALLATION SOUTH OF ISRAEL - DAY

SUPERIMPOSE: UNDERGROUND MILITARY INSTALLATION SOUTH OF
                    ISRAEL

SOUTHERN TECHNICIANS before missile control panels look greatly confused and alarmed as some are flipping switches by their monitors, trying to figure out what's really going on. They are Yemenize born.

INT. KNESSET - FLOOR - DAY

The politicians look furious as they turn to each other and talk inaudibly, discussing about the attack. The Knesset Prime Minister angrily throws his fist in the air.

                    KNESSET PRIME MINISTER
          The Southern Powers must be held
          accountable for this action. Tel
          Aviv must stand!

                    KNESSET MEMBERS
          We must retaliate!

INT. HAYWARD ENTERPRISES - STAGE - NIGHT

Hayward is laughing as his eyes are fixated on the video
screen.

ON VIDEO SCREEN

A map of the Middle east appears. No lines delineating
countries and no labels. A missile is being launched. A
tracking line originates in Tel Aviv. It travels to where the
third missile was launched south of Israel, followed by an
illustration of the explosion.

INT. SOUTHERN MILITARY INSTALLATION OUTSIDE OF ISRAEL - DAY

An explosion rocks the bunker. Plumes of dust mixed with
large chunks of debris fall down from the ceiling, injuring
some of the Southern Technicians. They panic as cracks widen
in the ceiling above their heads.

EXT. HAYWARD ENTERPRISES - STAGE - NIGHT

Cheers erupt from Hayward's audience. Hayward turns to face
his audience and applauds while holding his baton in one
hand. Soon after, he turns his attention back on the video
screen, watching with excitement in his eyes.

                    HAYWARD
          Not too happy, are they?

Hayward chuckles.

ON SCREEN

YEMEN BORN LEADER of the Southern Powers sits astride his
grand horse like a Sheik before his armies.

                    YEMEN BORN LEADER
          We attack Israel!

EXT. SOUTH OF ISRAEL - DAY

SUPERIMPOSE: STRONGHOLD OF THE SOUTHERN POWERS

Southern Armies move out. Camels and horses.

INT. HAYWARD ENTERPRISES - STAGE - NIGHT

Cheers erupt from the audience again. Hayward is bowing.

                    HAYWARD
          Oh, don't give me all the credit,
          guys.
                    (narcissistically)
          Yes, do.

INT. PENTAGON PLANNING ROOM - NIGHT

SUPERIMPOSE: PENTAGON

GENERALS are standing around a conference room table in
discussion. Documents being reviewed cover the table. Three
video screens on a wall show the progress of the Northern,
Eastern, and Southern Powers.

                    FIVE STAR GENERAL
          Looks like they are converging on
          Israel.

                    JUNIOR GENERAL
          Your orders?

The Five Star General pounds his fist into the table
defiantly.

EXT. CYPRUS - DAY

SUPERIMPOSE: OFF THE CYPRUS COAST

WESTERN POWERS MARINES scramble. A Western carrier fleet is
en route to Israel. State-of-the-art fighter jets fly
overhead.

EXT. ISRAEL - HAIFA AIRPORT - DAY

SUPERIMPOSE: HAIFA AIRPORT, ISRAEL

Soldiers from the Western Powers in high-tech fighting gear
disembark military transports and travel on foot across the
tarmac to awaiting military vehicles.

EXT. DESERT OUTSIDE HAIFA - DAY

Military vehicles caravan slowly move across the desert. A
GROUP OF WESTERN SOLDIERS marches alongside. A SARGENT (45)
leads them. A NERD-LIKE SOLDIER (18) struggles to keep up
with all the high-tech gear he is wearing. The Sargent
notices him.

                    SARGENT
          Try to keep up, son.

The Sargent adjusts his own high-tech gear, appearing
frustrated with it.

A NORTHERN POWERS MILITARY UNIT ambush them. Several western
military vehicles get hit. The Group Of Western Soldiers take
cover behind a burnt vehicle and attempt to respond.

INT. HAYWARD ENTERPRISES - STAGE - NIGHT

Hayward lifts his baton and points again at The Instigator.
The Instigator begins to code, typing rapidly.

ON SCREEN

EXT. CYPRUS

Western carrier fleet stalls in the water. Fighter jets
careen out of the sky.

BACK TO SCENE

Hayward is laughing on stage.

                    HAYWARD
          I did it! I did it! They're just
          dropping out of the sky.

The audience is cheering. Hayward feigns sorrow.

                    HAYWARD (CONT'D)
          Awww. Boo hoo.

More boisterous cheering and laughing erupt in the audience.

EXT. DESERT OUTSIDE HAIFA - DAY

Northern Powers Military Unit soldiers fire on The Group of
Western Soldiers.

The Group of Western Soldiers attempts to return fire with
their state-of-the-art weapons, but the weapons won't fire.
Confused looks cross their faces.

The Nerd-like Soldier attempts to use his high-tech gear to
assess the attack. He tries several instruments, then looks
up at the approaching Sargent.

                    SOLDIER
          The gear's disabled, Sargent. I
          can't use anything.

                    SARGENT
          We're blind?

The Sargent throws off his high-tech gear. Pulls an old
pistol out of his bag. His men gather around him hunkered
down. The Sargent stands, facing the enemy.

                    SARGENT (CONT'D)
          This hi-tech stuff's great, but you
          gotta rely on your gut. And this...

The Sargent runs while brandishing his pistol into the line
of fire from the Northern Armies Military Unit and falls
dead.

EXT. JERUSALEM - TEMPLE GROUNDS - 70 A.D. - NIGHT

Josephus attempts to get to Titus but is blocked by his
lieutenants who are gathering around him to celebrate.

Titus is chuckling. He makes no attempt to let Josephus reach
him. His lieutenants grin, sharing his amusement. Titus
feigns sorrow to them at the slain.

A riser is placed before Titus. He climbs onto it.

Titus then summons his soldiers, gesturing to them. They
gather around him. A DETACHMENT OF ROMANS SOLDIERS forms up.

                    TITUS
          You soldiers will be dispatched to
          Sanhedrin HQ.

Josephus follows them at a distance.

EXT. SANHEDRIN HQ - NIGHT

SUPERIMPOSE: JERUSALEM - SANHEDRIN OFFICES

Roman soldiers arrive. Josephus hurries behind them. They file in. Josephus stands reluctantly at the door. His eyes are filled with fear.

INT. SANHEDRIN HQ - NIGHT

Josephus watches on in horror as the soldiers slash the SANHEDRIN LEADERS to death. He stands by helplessly. Turns away. With a distraught look, Josephus runs off into the night. Wailing in the streets is heard.

EXT. NORTH OF ISRAEL - DAY

SUPERIMPOSE: SOMEWHERE NORTH OF ISRAEL - PRESENT DAY

Snow flies. Northern Armies snake south on horse and foot. Late model troop carriers and trucks move along the road.

EXT. EAST OF ISRAEL - DAY

SUPERIMPOSE: SOMEWHERE EAST OF ISRAEL

Along the mountain passes, the Eastern Armies progress on foot in vast numbers.

EXT. SOUTH OF ISRAEL - DAY

SUPERIMPOSE: SOMEWHERE SOUTH OF ISRAEL

Sand blows in the desert. The Southern Armies travel on horses and camels.

INT. BEDUIN TENT - DAY

SUPERIMPOSE: SOMEWHERE ON THE ARABIAN PENINSULA

Moscow Born Leader, Beijing Born Leader, and Yemen Born Leader are sharing a feast at an opulent low height table on oriental rugs with their respective FINANCE MINISTERS.

INT. NEW YORK - BANK BOARD ROOM - DAY

It's early morning. The digital clock on the wall reads: "6:00 AM."

A meeting is in progress in the opulent wood paneled board room of a bank in New York. Skyline view through a window.

WELL-DRESSED BANKERS are in urgent discussion. A global
financial crisis looms. Documents are open on the conference
table before them. BANKING ASSISTANTS ring the room on
laptops. Numerous video screens cover one wall with financial
data from around the world.

After prolonged discussion, ONE SENIOR BANKER stands and
holds up a $100 bill. He beckons everyone's attention. Then,
he dramatically rips it in half.

Well-Dressed Bankers and Banking Assistants look confused.

Then one "gets it" and smiles. Then another. Then they all
cheer him on! He picks up a pound note and rips it up and
does the same to the other currencies. More cheering erupts
after each rip. They all begin opening up their wallets and
purses and begin ripping.

INT. HAYWARD ENTERPRISES - STAGE - DAY

Hayward picks up his baton. He makes ready to conduct the
next part of the hacker's symphony. The music begins.

SUPERIMPOSE: THE CENTRAL BANKER'S MINUET

INTERCUT: Bank Board Room and Stage

Several of the Well-Dressed Bankers stand and dance a
"minuet" together. They move about the room gleefully.
Banking Assistants watch incredulously.

INT. HAYWARD ENTERPRISES - STAGE - DAY

                    HAYWARD
          Let's see what my hacker can do.

Hayward directs his attention to the hacker identified as The
Central Banker, who nods to Hayward and begins to type.

SUPERIMPOSE: THERE BEFORE ME WAS A BLACK HORSE! ITS RIDER WAS
            HOLDING A PAIR OF SCALES IN HIS HAND. THEN I
            HEARD, 'TWO POUNDS OF WHEAT FOR A DAY'S WAGES'

ON SCREEN

A montage of video scenes illustrates text line content below

INTERCUT - VIDEO SCENES AND THE TEXT LINES BELOW APPEARING
RAPIDLY IN SEQUENCE:

--CURRENCY MANIPULATION

--TARIFFS IMPOSED

--TRADE WAR BEGINS

--TRADE SLOWS

--SOVEREIGN DEBT INCREASES

--CORPORATE DEBT INCREASES

--PERSONAL DEBT INCREASES

--UNEMPLOYMENT RISES

--DEFAULTS MULTIPLY

--BANKRUPTCIES MULTIPLY

--STOCK MARKET PRICES TANK

--RUN ON BONDS

--GOLD HOARDING ENSUES

--ECONOMIES STAGNATE

--PLANTS CLOSE

--RETAIL STORES CLOSE

--TAXES INCREASE

--FINANCIAL TOOLS EXHAUSTED

--GOVERNMENT CAN'T BORROW

--UNRESTRAINED MONEY PRINTING COMMENCES GLOBALLY

--INFLATION SKYROCKETS

--DEPRESSION SINKS IN

--CIVIL UNREST

--MARAUDING GANGS OVERRUN POLICE

--RIOTS

...AND BREAD BECOMES TOO EXPENSIVE FOR ALL BUT THE VERY RICH.

INT. TEMPLE GROUNDS - NIGHT

Josephus arrives breathless and in a panic on the Temple
Grounds. The Temple is engulfed in flames.

Soldiers use battering rams and crow bars to disassemble the
remaining parts of the structure. Some soldiers are hauling
stone blocks away.

From afar, Josephus stands transfixed with horror as he
watches the chaos unfold. Chilling screams of women and
children can be heard in the background. Tears well up in his
eyes.

Innocent visitors to the city are being slaughtered
indiscriminately. Their bodies are sprawled in and around the
temple and blood flows down the temple steps. Rioters throw
torches into the temple accelerating the fire.

Josephus frantically searches the area.

                    JOSEPHUS
          Titus!

He finds Titus dining at a sumptuous table with his generals
on the temple grounds, watching the spectacle with pleasure.
The Menorah from the temple graces the middle of the table
like a candelabra.

Titus is munching on bread. Josephus approaches the table,
but the soldiers quickly grab him by the arms and restrain
him. He attempts to speak. A soldier punches him in the face.

                    TITUS
               (mockingly)
          I had hoped to preserve Herod's
          Temple as a Roman Pantheon of
          sorts. Pity.

Titus puts a hand on the Menorah.

                    TITUS (CONT'D)
          I'll have to settle for this ...and
          bring it back to Rome for my
          victory procession.
               (beat)
          Isn't it exciting?

Josephus rouses and glares at him.

Titus claps his hands a few times, summoning an underling. He
whispers instructions into the underling. More battering rams
are brought into place before the temple. Josephus watches
on in sorrow. Titus relishes his misery.

INT. HAYWARD ENTERPRISES - STAGE - DAY

Hayward picks up his baton.

                    HAYWARD
          Now to the final movement of the
          hacker's symphony...

SUPERIMPOSE: THE GRIM REAPER'S ALLEGRO

Hayward directs his attention to the hacker identified as The
Grim Reaper. The Grim Reaper begins to type.

SUPERIMPOSE: THERE BEFORE ME WAS A PALE HORSE! ITS RIDER WAS
             NAMED DEATH, AND HADES WAS FOLLOWING CLOSE
             BEHIND HIM. THEY WERE GIVEN POWER OVER A FOURTH
             OF THE EARTH TO KILL BY SWORD, FAMINE AND
             PLAGUE, AND BY THE WILD BEASTS OF THE EARTH.

ON SCREEN

A montage of video scenes illustrates text line content below

INTERCUT - VIDEO SCENES AND TEXT LINES BELOW APPEARING
RAPIDLY IN SEQUENCE:

--GLOBAL WARMING

--OCEAN LEVELS RISE

--EARTHQUAKES

--HURRICANES

--TSUNAMIS

--POLLUTION UNCHECKED

--VIRUSES AND BACTERIA PROLIFERATE

--PLAGUES AND DISEASE

--PREDATORY ANIMALS ESCAPE CAPTIVITY

--RATS BREED DISEASE

--SUPER-BUGS MULTIPLY

--INSECTS DESTROY THE FOOD SUPPLY

--WEAPONS OF MASS DESTRUCTION EMPLOYED

--MASSIVE RADIATION EXPOSURE

--SOCIETY BREAKS DOWN

--HOSPITALS ABANDONED

...ONE QUARTER OF THE EARTH DIES.

EXT. UNITED NATIONS - DAY

Helicopter view of the United Nations building.

INT. UNITED NATIONS ASSEMBLY HALL - DAY

ASSEMBLY MEMBERS are engaged in random heated discussions all
over the hall. No one is at the podium.

COALITION LEADER of the Western Powers gets up on his desk
and attempts to draw the attention of the Assembly Members.

INT. ASSEMBLY HALL MEDIA OBSERVATION ROOM - DAY

U.N. TECHNICIANS monitor a bank of video screens focused on
different areas of the Assembly Hall.

ON SCREEN #1

The Coalition Leader attempts unsuccessfully to draw
attention. He is wearing a name tag that reads: "WESTERN
POWERS."

INT. UNITED NATIONS ASSEMBLY HALL - DAY

The Coalition Leader is met with loud jeering and booing.
Several pens are being hurled at him from the crowd, hitting
him in the chest. His face is red with anger. He reluctantly
climbs down off his desk, then gathers the other WESTERN
POWER ASSEMBLY MEMBERS around him.

INT. ASSEMBLY HALL MEDIA OBSERVATION ROOM - DAY

U.N. Technicians continue to monitor a bank of video screens
focused on different areas of the Assembly Hall.

ON SCREEN #2

OPPOSING COALITION LEADERS of the Northern, Eastern, and
Southern Powers are moving their members together at one side
of the Assembly Hall. Each of the leaders wears a name tag.

Tags read respectively: NORTHERN POWERS, EASTERN POWERS, SOUTHERN POWERS.

INT. UNITED NATIONS ASSEMBLY HALL - DAY

Shouting and arguments ensue across the hall between the Assembly Hall Members. Some are angrily pointing fingers at each other, getting in each other's faces.

Dr. Frank Paulsen slowly climbs the stage to the podium. All eyes begin to turn to him. They calm down. Silence falls.

                    DR. FRANK PAULSEN
          Let's reorganize the world, shall
          we?
               (beat)
          A new world order.

Slowly, smiles and affirmations multiply across the hall. Assembly Members gather as one.

                    ASSEMBLY MEMBER #1
               (shouts)
          You lead us!

                    ASSEMBLY MEMBER #2
          Yeah!

The Assembly Members turn to each other and nod in agreement, acclaiming Dr. Paulsen as their leader.

EXT. ISRAEL - VALLEY OF JEZREEL - DAY

SUPERIMPOSE: ISRAEL - VALLEY OF JEZREEL - MEGIDDO

The Northern, Eastern, and Southern Armies gather on a vast plateau, using it as military staging area. A massive line of soldiers soon congeals and marches south to Jerusalem along the valley.

EXT. JERUSALEM - OUTSIDE THE SOUTHWEST BASE OF CITY WALL - NIGHT

SUPERIMPOSE: JERUSALEM - OUTSIDE THE CITY WALLS - 70 A.D.

Blocks of stone are being heaved over the side of the city walls. They fall and crash randomly. Roman soldiers are seen peering from the top of wall. Several dead bodies of Sanhedrin members and temple priests are tossed over as well. ONE IS ALIVE, screaming as he falls to his death.

EXT. TEMPLE GROUNDS - NIGHT

Piles of smoldering furniture and debris are everywhere. Most of the walls of the temple are reduced to ruins. A few blocks remain. Josephus shuffles across the grounds.

Soldiers here and there finish the destruction. Off in the distance, Josephus sees Roman carts loaded with blocks to be thrown over the side into the valley.

                    JOSEPHUS
          What have I done...?

Josephus falls to the ground with tears running down his face. A group of Hellenizers stops and stares at Josephus in his misery.

                    HELLENIZER
          Josephus, you went too far with the
          Romans.

They each give him a scornful look, then walk off in disgust.

Titus then walks up with a contingent of soldiers. He pokes Josephus on the ground with his baton.

                    TITUS
          Get up. My father has summoned you
          to Rome. For what reason, I know
          not.

EXT. JERUSALEM - KIDRON VALLEY OUTSIDE THE CITY - DAY

SUPERIMPOSE: KIDRON VALLEY OUTSIDE THE OLD CITY - PRESENT DAY

Vast columns of soldiers enter the valley between the Mount of Olives and the Eastern Gate. It's a mixed company of Northern, Eastern, and Southern soldiers.

Residents living outside the city in their path flee in terror. Soldiers pillage as they go. They soon congeal at the foot of the Eastern Gate to the city and make camp.

EXT. JERUSALEM - ATOP THE OLD CITY WALLS - NIGHT

The population of the Old City in Jerusalem watches on in horror.

INT. JERUSALEM - INSPECTOR ERAS'S HOME - DINING ROOM - NIGHT

Inspector Eras, Mags, Ben, Emily, Agent Ariel, Agent Ariel'S
WIFE, INSPECTOR ERAS'S WIFE and DAUGHTER (12) are gathered
for a Passover Seder. Daughter is same actor as Josephus'
younger sister, Logan, now in the present day.

A table is set with fine silverware, plates, and wine
glasses. Each character is dressed in fine clothes. Inspector
Eras's Wife wears a white robe.

A Seder plate containing various symbolic foods is set before
her. Placed nearby is a plate with three matzot and dishes of
salt water for dipping.

                    INSPECTOR ERAS
          Exodus 13:8 reads, "You shall tell
          your child on that day, saying, 'It
          is because of what the LORD did for
          me when I came out of Egypt.'"

                    INSPECTOR ERAS'S WIFE
          And so, we perform the ritual of
          the Seder to remember.
               (to guests)
          Thank you for being with us for
          this celebration.

                    INSPECTOR ERAS
          We have adapted it somewhat,
          however, to our own beliefs in some
          very meaningful ways.

                    INSPECTOR ERAS'S WIFE
          Let us begin with the blessings and
          first cup of wine.

MONTAGE: The first cup of wine is shared; they all wash their
hands with a clean cloth, each one of them dips a piece of
celery in salt water and tastes it. Matzah bread is broken
and shared. Inspector Eras's Wife then appears to read a
story to the group. The montage ends...

Inspector Eras takes a large piece of matzoh, shows it to his
daughter, Logan, who smiles, and then hides it away in a
drawer to be retrieved later.

Inspector Eras sits again. He nods to the Daughter.

                    DAUGHTER
          Why is tonight different from all
          other nights?

                    INSPECTOR ERAS'S WIFE
          We eat only matzah because our
          ancestors could not wait for their
          breads to rise when they were
          fleeing slavery in Egypt, and so
          they were flat when they came out
          of the oven.

                    DAUGHTER
          Why is it that on all other nights
          we eat meat either roasted,
          marinated, or cooked, but on this
          night, it is entirely roasted?

                    INSPECTOR ERAS'S WIFE
          We eat only roasted meat because
          that is how the Passover lamb was
          prepared during sacrifice in the
          Temple at Jerusalem.

                    INSPECTOR ERAS
                (to Ben, Emily, and Mags)
          Our new addition to the ritual.

                    DAUGHTER
          But now the Temple is gone. What of
          the lamb?

                    INSPECTOR ERAS
          We look forward to the return of
          the Lamb of God who never needs to
          be sacrificed again.

A moment of silent reflection ensues.

                    INSPECTOR ERAS'S WIFE
          The second cup of wine.

They lift a second cup of wine and drink. They then wash
their hands again with a clean cloth.

                    INSPECTOR ERAS'S WIFE (CONT'D)
          And now the bitter herbs.

They pass the Seder plate and share grated horseradish mixed
with cooked beets and romaine lettuce.

                    INSPECTOR ERAS
          In Numbers 9:11, we are told to eat
          the lamb, together with the
          unleavened bread. We are also told
          to eat bitter herbs which symbolize
          the bitterness of our slavery in
          Egypt.

                    INSPECTOR ERAS'S WIFE
          And now the Shulchan Orech. We eat
          the fish.

They pass the Seder plate and each takes a piece of charred
egg.

Inspector Eras nods to his Daughter.

                    INSPECTOR ERAS
          And now the afikoman to finish our
          meal.

The Daughter retrieves the piece of matzah from the drawer
and brings it to her mother who breaks and distributes it to
the characters.

                    INSPECTOR ERAS'S WIFE
          Let us recite the Birkat Hamazon,
          or grace after a meal.

MONTAGE: The group appears to recite.

                    INSPECTOR ERAS'S WIFE
          The third cup of wine.

They each drink a cup of wine.

Inspector Eras's Wife refills the cups. She nods to her
Daughter.

                    INSPECTOR ERAS
          Please open the front door.

The Daughter opens the door then finds her seat again.

                    INSPECTOR ERAS (CONT'D)
          I read from Psalm 79:6-7.

As Inspector Eras reads:

EXT. JERUSALEM - NIGHT

MONTAGE: Armies of the world encamp before Jerusalem.

                    INSPECTOR ERAS (V.O.)
          Pour out your wrath on the nations
          that do not acknowledge you, on the
          kingdoms that do not call on your
          name; for they have devoured Jacob
          and devastated his homeland.

INT. JERUSALEM - INSPECTOR ERAS'S HOME - DINING ROOM - NIGHT

> INSPECTORS ERAS'S WIFE
> Miriam's Cup, the fourth and final
> cup.

Inspector Eras refills the cups. All raise their cups of
wine. They drink.

MONTAGE: The characters sing the Hallel. Then--

> INSPECTOR ERAS
> And now, the Nirtzah.
> > (beat)
> Next year, in Jerusalem.

> INSPECTOR ERAS'S WIFE
> Next year, in Jerusalem.

> DAUGHTER
> Or now, Daddy? Our Messiah?

All raise their cups of wine.

> ALL
> > (in unison)
> Now we pray! Our Messiah this year
> in Jerusalem!

INT. KNESSET - FLOOR - NEXT MORNING

Politicians assemble in the Knesset. A large video screen
shows the encamped armies. Politicians argue among
themselves. Some shake their fists at the screen.

Mags, Inspector Eras, Ben, and Emily are on the floor of the
Knesset, watching in horror.

A pair of politicians who favor the Prime Minister glare
disapprovingly at Inspector Eras.

The Messianic Coalition Leader abruptly takes the podium at
the Knesset and calls for attention. Knesset Prime Minister
eyes him uneasily.

Legislative Assistant encourages the Prime Minister to stop
him. Knesset Prime Minister declines to interfere in order to
appear open to all opinions during a crisis.

                    MESSIANIC COALITION LEADER
          Brothers and sisters, not since we
          were scattered to the world in the
          days of Josephus have we been a
          nation as we are today, together
          and free...

A titter of cheers across the room.

                    MESSIANIC COALITION LEADER (CONT'D)
          And, I, for one, am not willing to
          lose that for us as a nation again.
          If ever there was a time we needed
          Messiah its now!

A cascade of cheers fills the room. It builds to a crescendo.

INT. KNESSET - HALLWAY - DAY

Mags boldly gathers Inspector Eras, Ben, and Emily in a quiet
hallway of the floor of the Knesset.

                    MAGS
          There's a passage in Zechariah I
          remember learning in temple growing
          up.

                    EMILY
          In the Old Testament?

                    INSPECTOR ERAS
          In the Prophets. I know it.

                    BEN
          OK, what?

                    MAGS
          I think I know where we should be
          for the final showdown.
               (beat)
          I wish Brandon was here.

EXT. JERUSALEM - MILITARY TRAINING GROUND OUTSIDE THE OLD
CITY - NIGHT

SUPERIMPOSE: ISRAELI MILITARY

The Israel military prepares for the assault.

EXT. HAYWARD ENTERPRISES - DAY

Helicopter view of Hayward Enterprises.

INT. HAYWARD ENTERPRISES - LOBBY - DAY

Brandon enters the lobby. He surreptitiously pulls out Mags'
shielded wafer package, opens it, and replaces it in his
pocket. He approaches the security desk with overhead
scanner.

Holding his breath, he waves Mags' Employee pass quickly and
passes in with other employees. He walks with the group
towards the auditorium entrance.

As he walks, Brandon feels for the gun that is in his jacket
pocket.

INT. HAYWARD ENTERPRISES - STAGE - DAY

Hayward is on the stage bowing to the applauding audience.

Brandon finds a seat and sits with others.

Technician comes out from the wings and calls Hayward aside.
He whispers in his ear.

Hayward comes forward on the stage.

                    HAYWARD
          I understand my niece, Mags, is in
          the audience with us today. Mags?

Two security guards come up to Brandon's seat and usher him
up on the stage.

Hayward looks surprised.

                    HAYWARD (CONT'D)
          Why Mags, I always wondered about
          your gender preference. I like you
          better as a man.

Brandon feels in his pocket.

                    BRANDON
          Where is Mags?

                    HAYWARD
          The pit of hell for all I care.
          She's a traitor. And, dead to me.

INT. PRESS ROOM OVERLOOKING THE STAGE - DAY

The DIRECTOR turns to the VIDEOGRAPHER and snaps his fingers,
rushing him.

                    DIRECTOR
          Let's get this.

The Videographer hurriedly switches on her camera and aims it
at the action.

                    DIRECTOR (CONT'D)
          Are we rolling?

The Videographer nods. Video appears on MEDIA TECHNICIAN'S
monitor. Media Technician nods.

INT. HAYWARD ENTERPRISES - STAGE - DAY

                    BRANDON
          You're her uncle!

                    HAYWARD
          She's helping a renegade nation,
          Israel, defy the new world order!

He directs attention to the hackers.

                    HAYWARD (CONT'D)
          Any action we take to stop her and
          her new homeland are warranted,
          including utilizing these good
          people.

Audience cheers. Hayward parades around the stage then gets
in Brandon's face, preparing to say something.

Brandon reaches in his pocket, pulls out the gun, and puts
the barrel to Hayward's forehead. He shoots point blank. POP!

                    BRANDON
          You are one ...evil ...dude.

Hayward falls flat on his back. Brandon turns to the
audience.

                    BRANDON (CONT'D)
                (to the audience)
          He's capable of anything!

A DOCTOR in the crowd runs up and checks Hayward's pulse at
his neck.

There's a large bullet hole in Hayward's forehead.

The Doctor shakes his head.

                         DOCTOR
              He's dead.

The Doctor looks at his watch for the time.

Loud wailing and shouts of "No!" begin in the audience.

INT. PRESS ROOM OVERLOOKING THE STAGE - DAY

The Director turns to the MEDIA TECHNICIAN.

                         DIRECTOR
              This going out to everybody?

A bank of monitors shows internet and network TV cameras are
live with the action on the stage worldwide.

Media Technician nods.

INT. HAYWARD ENTERPRISES - STAGE - DAY

Dr. Paulsen hurries out on stage from the wings. He kneels
next to Hayward. Dramatically, Dr. Paulsen picks up Hayward's
lifeless hand. Hackers stand and bow their heads in unison.

Security Guards come up behind Brandon and disarm him.

Brandon chucks the wafer and employee pass on Hayward's
lifeless body as the Security Guards remove him from the
stage.

Audience rustles.

Moments later, Hayward's lifeless hand squeezes Dr.
Paulsen's. Dr. Paulsen smiles subtly.

Hayward sits up.

The audience gasps.

The bullet wound on Hayward's forehead miraculously heals
before the world's eyes.

INT. PRESS ROOM OVERLOOKING THE STAGE - DAY

Internet and TV cameras continue live, capturing the action on the stage worldwide. The Director and Media Technician stare at the monitors.

                    DIRECTOR
               (turns to Media
                Technician)
          What just happened?

                    MEDIA TECHNICIAN
          A resurrection? No way.

INT. HAYWARD ENTERPRISES - STAGE - DAY

Hayward tries to rise to his feet. Dr. Paulsen helps him. He finally stands, rubs his head, and smiles.

                    HAYWARD
          I guess I _am_ capable of anything.

Dr. Paulsen takes Hayward's hand and raises it high in the air in a victory move.

                    DR. FRANK PAULSEN
          I give you Richard Hayward, Son of
          the Morning, who will usher in the
          dawn of Pax Dyrette for the world!

Wild cheers fill the room. Hayward and Dr. Paulsen stand side by side facing the audience and bow to massive applause and cheering.

EXT. HAYWARD ENTERPRISES - REAR LOADING DOCK - DAY

As security guards prepare to haul Brandon away, Agent Ariel and Female Agent intercept them, taking out the guards. They spirit Brandon away in their unmarked vehicle.

INT. VEHICLE - DAY

Brandon ducks down in the back seat.

                    BRANDON
          Who are you guys?

Agent Ariel and Female Agent exchange a look.

                    AGENT
          (in thick Israeli accent)
     The guys ...who are going to take
     you to Mags.

The Female Agent holds up a cell phone.

                    FEMALE AGENT
     You want to talk to her?

                    BRANDON
     Is it secure?

                    FEMALE AGENT
     As secure as Mags can make it.

Brandon takes the cell phone. Listens.

INT. ISRAELI SECURITY SUV - DAWN

Mags, Ben, Emily, and Inspector Eras are in the SUV's
passenger seats. Sitting up front is the Driver. The passing
highway sign seen through windshield reads: "BEN GURION
AIRPORT."

Mags holds the cell phone to her ear.

                    MAGS
          (into cell phone)
     Brandon?

                    BRANDON (V.O.)
     Mags! Mags! So good to hear you
     voice!
          (beat)
     It's over.

                    MAGS
          (into cell phone)
     Not so sure about that...

                    BRANDON (V.O.)
     Where are you?

                    MAG
          (into cell phone)
     In Israel. It's almost morning
     here. We're on our way to meet
     you...

Connection is lost. There's dead silence.

EXT. JERUSALEM - KIDRON VALLEY OUTSIDE THE CITY - DAY

Soldiers mill about, waiting for orders.

SUPERIMPOSE: HOURS LATER

A massive rushing sound is heard. Dark clouds roll in.
Soldiers look skywards. Lightning strikes. Rushing sound
intensifies. Lightning intensifies.

SUPERIMPOSE: I WILL GATHER ALL THE NATIONS TO JERUSALEM TO
FIGHT AGAINST IT ...THEN THE LORD WILL GO OUT AND FIGHT
AGAINST THOSE NATIONS, AS HE FIGHTS ON A DAY OF BATTLE.

Sounds of concrete scraping over concrete and stone scraping
over stone are heard.

An eerie background chorus of human howling and lamentation
pervades the air.

SUPERIMPOSE: AND ON THAT DAY HIS FEET WILL STAND ON THE MOUNT
OF OLIVES, EAST OF JERUSALEM, AND THE MOUNT OF OLIVES WILL BE
SPLIT IN TWO FROM EAST TO WEST ...

An explosive cracking sound splits the air; the rumbling of
an earthquake.

SUPERIMPOSE: THEN THE LORD MY GOD WILL COME, AND ALL THE HOLY
ONES WITH HIM.

Then, the dark clouds rapidly part. Bright sunshine explodes
through the opening onto the assembled armies.

Some soldiers drop their weapons and fall to their knees.
Others stand firm with looks of defiance.

EXT. JERUSALEM - ATOP THE OLD CITY WALLS - DAY

The population of Jerusalem lets out a mighty cheer.

INT. ROME - COUNTY ESTATE OF JOSEPHUS - GARDEN ROOM - DAY

SUPERIMPOSE: ROME - 98 A.D.

Old Josephus is writing in his diary. He reads to himself
what he has written.

                    OLD JOSEPHUS
          Many see me as a traitor to the
          Jewish people, my people, but that
          is not so.
                    (MORE)

                    OLD JOSEPHUS (CONT'D)
          I told you I would reveal my true
          motive for conspiring with the
          Romans. It was not for revenge,
          cowardice, or personal gain. It
          was because I wanted to turn the
          hearts of my people away from faith
          in temple sacrifice to the messiah
          for their salvation.
                    (beat)
          You see, I believed the two monks.

EXT. HIGH POINT OF THE KIDRON VALLEY OPPOSITE THE EASTERN
GATE OF THE OLD CITY - DAY

Winds gather into a localized cyclone. Lightning emanates.
Thunder crashes. Then...

UNSEEN MESSIAH'S POV: Hovering just above the ground, slowly
moving down into the Kidron Valley, crossing over empty
ancient tombs, over soldiers, and over the steps outside the
walled up Eastern (Golden) Gate, then entering the city after
the Eastern Gate vaporizes.

EXT. JERUSALEM - KIDRON VALLEY OUTSIDE THE CITY - DAY

The armies of the world lay down their arms awestruck.

EXT. JERUSALEM - OLD CITY - DAY

UNSEEN MESSIAH'S POV: High in the sky above the old city, a
nebulous temple-like structure slowly descends, translucent
and glowing. We can just barely make it out.

The population of Jerusalem gathers and watches.

UNSEEN MESSIAH'S POV: Rises to meet it, then fades.

The Israeli Security SUV speeds to where it is descending and
stops. Mags, Inspector Eras, Agent Ariel, Ben, Emily, and
Brandon jump out and look up awestruck. Brandon and Mags
delighted to be reunited.

Another SUV pulls up behind them and the Messianic Coalition
Leader and Others With Him jump out and join them. Other cast
member gather around.

They all exchange smiles of joy as they watch. Inspector Eras
weeps.

                                        FADE OUT.   *

*